CLASH OF CIVILIZATIONS OVER AN ELEVATOR IN PIAZZA VITTORIO

Amara Lakhous

CLASH OF CIVILIZATIONS OVER AN ELEVATOR IN PIAZZA VITTORIO

*Translated from the Italian
by Ann Goldstein*

Europa
editions

Europa Editions
116 East 16th Street
New York, N.Y. 10003
www.europaeditions.com
info@europaeditions.com

Translation by Ann Goldstein
Original title: *Scontro di civiltà per un ascensore a piazza Vittorio*
Translation copyright © 2008 by Europa Editions

Library of Congress Cataloging in Publication Data is available
ISBN 978-1-933372-61-7

Lakhous, Amara
Clash of Civilizations Over an Elevator in Piazza Vittorio

Book design by Emanuele Ragnisco
www.mekkanografici.com

Cover illustration by Chiara Carrer

Prepress by Plan.ed – Rome

Printed in the United States of America

CONTENTS

For Roberto De Angelis
With affection and gratitude

"Can't you have a little patience?"
"No!"
Because the southerner, my dear sir, wants to be what he was not, wants to encounter two things: the truth, and the faces of those who are absent."

The Southerner
AMAL DONKOL (1940-83)

The truth is at the bottom of a well: look into a well and you see the sun or the moon; but throw yourself down and there is neither sun nor moon, there is the truth.

The Day of the Owl
LEONARDO SCIASCIA (1921-89)

Happy people have neither age nor memory, they have no need of the past.

The Invention of the Desert
TAHAR DJAOUT (1954-93)

THE TRUTH ACCORDING
TO PARVIZ MANSOOR SAMADI

A few days ago—it was barely eight o'clock in the morning—sitting in the metro, rubbing my eyes and fighting sleep because I'd woken up so early, I saw an Italian girl devouring a pizza as big as an umbrella. I felt so sick to my stomach I almost threw up. Thank goodness she got out at the next stop. It was really a disgusting sight! The law should punish people who feel free to disturb the peace of good citizens going to work in the morning and home at night. The damage caused by people eating pizza in the metro is a lot worse than the damage caused by cigarettes. I hope that the proper authorities do not underestimate this sensitive issue and will proceed immediately to put up signs like "Pizza Eating Prohibited," next to the ones that are so prominent at the metro entrances saying "No Smoking!" I would just like to know how Italians manage to consume such a ridiculous amount of dough morning and evening.

My hatred for pizza is beyond compare, but that doesn't mean that I hate everyone who eats it. I'd like things to be clear right from the start: I don't hate the Italians.

What I'm saying is not beside the point—far from it. I really am talking about Amedeo. Please be patient with me. As you know, Amedeo is my only friend in Rome, in fact he's more than a friend—it's no exaggeration to say that I love him the way I love my brother Abbas. I really love Amedeo, even though he's a pizza addict. As you see, my hatred for pizza doesn't come from hostility toward Italians.

In fact, it's not important whether Amedeo is Italian or not. My concern is to avoid at all costs the consequences of my aversion to pizza. For example, a few weeks ago I was fired from my job as a dishwasher in a restaurant near Piazza Navona when the owner happened to find out that I hate pizza. Bastards. An outrage like that, and there are still people who maintain that freedom of taste, expression, and religion, not to mention democracy, are guaranteed in this country! I would like to know: does the law punish pizza-haters? If the answer is yes, we've got a real scandal here; if the answer is no, then I am entitled to compensation.

Don't be in such a hurry. Allow me to tell you that your biggest failing is hurry. Your watchword is impatience. You drink coffee the way cowboys drink whiskey. Coffee is like tea, you should avoid gulping it down—it should be sipped. Amedeo is like hot tea on a cold day. No, Amedeo is like the taste of fruit at the end of a meal, after you've had bruschetta with tomatoes or olives, then the notorious first course, which includes all those different pastas I can't stand, like spaghetti and company (ravioli, fettuccine, lasagna, fusilli, orecchiette, rigatoni, and so on), and finally the second course, of meat or fish with side dishes of vegetables. All things I've gotten to know from my occasional jobs in Italian restaurants. I really love fruit, so don't be surprised if I compare Amedeo to fruit. Let's say Amedeo is as sweet as a grape. The juice of the grape is so good!

It's pointless to persist with this question: is Amedeo Italian? Whatever the answer is, it won't solve the problem. But then who is Italian? Only someone who was born in Italy, has an Italian passport and identity card, knows the language, has an Italian name, and lives in Italy? As you see, the question is very complicated. I'm not saying that Amedeo is an enigma. Rather, he's like a poem by Omar Khayyam: you need a lifetime to understand its meaning, and only then will your heart open to the world and tears warm your cold cheeks. Now, at least, it's enough for you to know that Amedeo knows Italian better than millions of Italians scattered like locusts to the four corners of the earth. I'm not drunk. I didn't mean to offend you.

I don't despise locusts; in fact, I respect them, because they procure their food with dignity—they don't count on anyone. And then it's certainly not my fault if the Italians like to travel and to emigrate. Even today I'm amazed when I hear speeches by certain Italian politicians on the news and on television programs. Take, for example, Roberto Bossosso.

You don't know who Roberto Bossosso is? He's the leader of the Forza Nord party, which considers all Muslim immigrants enemies. Every time I hear his voice, I'm assailed by doubts; I look around in bewilderment and ask the first person I see, "That language Bossosso speaks—is that really Italian?" Up to now I haven't gotten any satisfactory answers. Often people will say to me: "You don't know Italian," or "First, you have to learn the language better," or "Sorry, but your Italian is very poor." Usually I hear these poisonous phrases when I'm looking for work as a restaurant cook and in the end they shunt me into the kitchen to wash dishes. "It seems that the only thing you know how to do, dear Parviz, is wash dishes!" Stefania likes to provoke me and tease me like that. There's no question that she's disappointed in me, since she was the first person who taught me Italian, or, to be more precise, tried to teach me. I'm not

Amedeo, that's as clear as a star in the peaceful sky of Shiraz. But I'm sorry to inform you that I'm not the only one who doesn't know Italian in this country. I've worked in restaurants in Rome with a lot of young Neapolitans, Calabrians, and Sicilians, and I've discovered that our language level is about the same. Mario, the cook in the restaurant at the Termini station, wasn't wrong when he said: "Remember, Parviz, we're all foreigners in this city!" I've never in my life seen anyone like Mario: he drinks wine like water, and it has no effect on him.

O.K., I'll tell you about Mario the Neapolitan some other time. Now you want to know everything about Amedeo—that is, start dinner with dessert? As you wish. The customer is king. I still remember the first time I saw him. He was sitting in one of the desks in the first row near the blackboard. I approached; there was an empty seat near his, I smiled and sat down next to him after saying the only Italian word I knew—"Ciao!" This word is really helpful, you use it when you're saying hello to someone and when you're saying goodbye. There's another word that's just as important: cock. It's used to express rage and to calm down, and males don't have a monopoly on it. Even Benedetta, the old concierge, uses it all the time, without embarrassment. Speaking of which, old Benedetta is the concierge of the building where Amedeo lives, in Piazza Vittorio. This wretched woman has a nasty habit of lurking near the elevator, ready to pick a fight with anyone who wants to use it. I adore the elevator, I don't take it because I'm lazy—I meditate in it. You press the button without any effort, you go up or descend, it could even break down while you're inside. It's exactly like life, full of breakdowns. Now you're up, now you're down. I was up . . . in Paradise . . . in Shiraz, living happily with my wife and children, and now I'm down . . . in Hell, suffering from homesickness. The elevator is a tool for meditation. As I told you, it's a practice I'm used to: going up and coming down is a mental exercise like yoga. Unfortunately Benedetta watches me like a cantankerous cat, and as soon as I set foot in the elevator she yells at me: "*Guaglio'! Guaglio'!*"[1]

"*Guaglio'*" is Benedetta's favorite word. As you know, *guaglio'* means "fuck" in Neapolitan. At least, that's what a lot of Neapolitans I've worked with have told me. Every time she sees me head for the elevator she starts shouting, "*Guaglio'! Guaglio'! Guaglio'!*" In Iran, it's customary to show respect for old people and avoid bad words. That's why, instead of answering the insult with another insult, I confine myself to a brief response: "*Merci!*" I leave and go away without looking at her. By the way, you know that *merci* is a French word that means "thank you"? Amedeo told me, he knows French well.

I met him at a free Italian class for immigrants in Piazza Vittorio. I had just arrived in Rome. Amedeo was different from the others because he went to all of Stefania's classes, he didn't miss a single one. At first I didn't understand why he was so diligent and so good. But passion is like the shining sun and no one can resist its rays, passion is youth's best friend. There's a Persian proverb that goes: youth is as intoxicating as wine. A few months later Amedeo decided to go and live with Stefania in her apartment, which overlooks the gardens of Piazza Vittorio, and he also stopped coming to school, since he didn't need lessons for beginners, the way I did. But we stayed in touch; we met almost every day at Sandro's bar to have a cappuccino or a cup of tea. Sandro

[1] Literally, "boy."

is a nice man, but he gets mad easily. All you have to say is "Go Lazio!" to make him furious, whereas if you're a fan of the Rome team he treats you like an old friend. Once he asked me if there were any Rome fans in Iran, and not to disappoint him I said, "Of course," and then he hugged me.

Obviously I also saw Amedeo at his house. I'm very fond of his small kitchen. It's the only place that brings solace to my aching heart. When I think of my children, Shadi, Said, Surab, and Omar, and my wife, Zeinab, I get very sad. Where are they now? Wandering, I suppose, God knows where. How I wish I could kiss them and hug them. Only tears and these bottles of Chianti put out the fires of longing. I cry a lot and I drink even more, to forget my ordeals. I got into the habit of going every day to sit near the fountain across from the entrance to the church of Santa Maria Maggiore to feed the pigeons and cry. No one can take the Chianti away from me except Amedeo, he's the only one who dares pull me out of the hell of my grief. He sits beside me in silence, lets me cry and drink for a few minutes, then suddenly he gets up as if a snake had bitten him, and says to me in a tone of confusion: "My God, we're late! We have to make dinner, Stefania's having a party. Did you forget, Parviz?" He always says the same words, in the same way, with the same seriousness. I look at him and laugh until I'm exhausted, laughing helps me breathe. In the meantime Amedeo confounds me with jokes so hilarious that we laugh like lunatics in front of the tourists. Before we go to his house we stop at Iqbal the Bangladeshi's shop in Piazza Vittorio to buy what we need for the party: rice, chicken, spices, fruit, beer, and wine. I take a shower and change, and there is Amedeo opening the kitchen door: "Welcome to your kingdom, Shahryar, great sultan of Persia!" He closes the door and leaves me alone for hours. I immediately start preparing Iranian dishes, like *gormeh sabzi* and *kubideh kebab*, *kashk badenjan* and *kateh*. The odors that fill the kitchen make me forget reality and I imagine that I've returned to my kitchen in Shiraz. After a while the perfume of the spices is transformed into incense, and this makes me dance and sing like a dervish, ahi, ahi, ahi . . . In a few minutes the kitchen is in a Sufi trance. When I finish cooking I open the door and find the guests waiting for me in the living room. Then the party begins.

Each of us has a place where we feel comfortable. For some it's a church, for some a mosque, a sanctuary, a movie theater, a stadium, a market. I feel comfortable in a kitchen. And it's not that surprising, because I'm a good cook. It's a skill that was handed down to me from my grandfather and my father. I'm not a dishwasher, as they say in the restaurants of Rome. In Shiraz I had a good restaurant. Damn those bastards who ruined me, in the blink of an eye I lost everything: family, house, restaurant, money. People keep telling me: "If you want to work as a chef in Italy you have to learn the secrets of Italian cooking." What can I do if I can't bear pizza and spaghetti and company? Anyway, it's pointless to learn Italian cooking. Soon I'm going back to Shiraz. I know I am.

I wonder why the Italian authorities continue to deny what all honest doctors know: pasta makes people fat, and causes obesity. The fat gradually starts to block the arteries until the poor heart stops beating. It even happened to Elvis. You remember how thin and handsome he was when he sang *"Baba bluma bib bab a blue . . ."* In those days, he ate rice every day, but then, unfortunately, he got used to pizza that he ordered in from the Italian restaurants in Hollywood, because he didn't have time to cook, to sit down at the table and eat. Poor Elvis had too many commitments, and the result was that in a short time he got as fat as an elephant and died—the fat saturated his heart, his lungs, his eyes, his whole body. No one can contain that deluge of fat. I've warned Maria Cristina, the home health aide, not to eat pasta. When I met her two years ago, she was thin, too, then she got used to spaghetti and blew up like a hot-air balloon. Once I said to her, "Why have you abandoned your roots—isn't rice the favorite food of Filipinos?" Poor Maria Cristina, recently they decided to forbid her to use the elevator, out of fear she'd break it. "You weigh more than three people put together"—that's how they justified keeping her out. So why doesn't the ministry of health add to the labels of pasta packages the words "Seriously hazardous to your health"?

Amedeo is like a beautiful harbor from which we depart and to which we always return. When I'm sacked from a job I'm like a person who's been shipwrecked, and Amedeo's the only one who helps me out. He always says to me: "Don't worry, Parviz, come on, let's have a look at *Porta Portese.*" And so we sit in Sandro's bar. Amedeo opens the paper and marks the important ads with a little x, then we go to his house to make the phone calls. I stare at him in astonishment, like a child looking at a rainbow. Amedeo is amazing. I listen to him speaking his elegant Italian. After a few phone calls he takes the *TuttoCittà*, the city guide, and glances at the pages to be sure of the exact street names, makes some notes in his notebook, and then looks at me and says, "The restaurants of Rome await you, Signor Parviz!" We go together to see the restaurant owners, and obviously I say nothing—I let Amedeo speak for me. He's so convincing, fantastic! Very often I start work that same day as an assistant cook, even if a few days later I'm packed off to wash dishes. It's hard for me to take orders in the kitchen. I hate being assistant cook, I prefer to wash dishes and put up with the pain in my back and a bit of arthritis rather than take orders: "Parvis, peel the onion!" "Parvis, put the water on!," "Parviz, prepare the pasta!," "Parviz, get the carrots from the refrigerator!," "Parviz, check the spaghetti!," "Parviz, wash the fruit!," "Parviz, clean the fish!" For me the kitchen is like a ship. Parviz Mansoor Samadi doesn't set foot on a ship unless he's in command, that's the truth. Amedeo always goes with me to any administrative proceeding, like renewing my residency permit, or dealing with other bureaucratic matters . . . When I went to the city offices by myself I'd lose control at the drop of a hat, and start shouting, and they'd throw me out every time like a mangy dog. They'd yell things like "If you come back here again we'll call the police!" I don't know why they always threaten to call the police!

Where is he now? Who knows. All I know is that Amedeo will leave a terrible hole in our lives. In fact, I can't imagine Rome without Amedeo. I still remember that wretched day in the police station on Via Genova, where I had gone to pick up the decision from the High Commissioner for Refugees. The words of the police inspector shocked me: "Your petition has been rejected, all you can do is appeal." I went into the first bar I came to on the street, bought some bottles of Chianti, I don't remember how many, and headed for Santa Maria Maggiore to sit near the fountain, as usual, but that time I went to drink and weep. I was devastated that my petition had been rejected, because I'm not a liar. I fled Shiraz because I was threat-

ened, if I go back to Iran there'll be a noose waiting for me.
They took me for a fraud and a liar. But it had never crossed
my mind to leave Iran. During the war against Iraq I fought
in the front lines and was wounded several times. And then
why would I abandon my children, my wife, my house, my
restaurant, and Shiraz, except to avoid being killed! I'm a
refugee, not an immigrant.

Ah no! This is an important fact, it has to do with my
friend Amedeo. I told you, I wept for a long time, and I
drank a lot of wine, and then I had a clever idea. I went back
to the welcome center where I lived, got a needle and
thread, and carried out my plan. I still remember the social
worker's cries: "Oh my God, Parviz has sewed up his
mouth!" "Oh God, Parviz has sewed up his mouth!" Many
people intervened, they tried to persuade me to back down,
but I refused. They called an ambulance, the doctor tried to
make me stop, but it was useless. After several attempts,
lasting for hours, they called the cops, who tried by every
possible means to take me to the hospital. But I resisted
with all my might. I closed my eyes and it seemed to me that
I was sleeping near the mausoleum of Hafiz in Shiraz, the
way I did as a child. I made a tremendous effort to convince
myself that everything that was happening was just a bad
dream or a delirium caused by alcohol. Then I opened my
eyes to a policeman who was shouting and waving his club,
saying: "Either you go to the emergency room on your own
or we put you in a straitjacket and take you to the psychi-
atric ward." I said to myself, "The only way I'll move from
here is inside a coffin." I closed my eyes again as if I were a
corpse. At some point I felt a warm hand, and I struggled to
open my eyes. In front of me I saw Amedeo. It was the first
time I'd seen him cry. He embraced me the way a mother

embraces her child who's trembling with cold because he was caught by surprise in the rain on the way home from school. I cried for a long time in his arms, in a flood of tears. When I stopped, Amedeo went with me to the emergency room, where they removed the thread from my mouth, and with great difficulty I started to breathe again. Amedeo insisted that I spend the night at his house. The truth is that Amedeo is the only one in this city who loves me.

It's impossible! Amedeo a murderer! I will never believe what you're telling me. I know him the way I know the taste of Chianti and *gormeh sabzi*. I'm sure he's innocent. What does Amedeo have to do with that thug who pisses in the elevator? I saw him with my own eyes, I said to him: "This is not a public toilet." He gave me a look of such hatred and said, "If you say that again I'll piss in your mouth! You're in my house, you have no right to speak! Get it, you piece of shit?" And then he kept shouting at me, right in my face: "Italy for Italians! Italy for Italians!" I didn't want to argue with him, because he's crazy. Have you ever heard of a sane man who shamelessly pees in the elevator and is called the Gladiator? Frankly I wasn't sorry about his death. That Gladiator kid isn't the only lunatic in the building. Amedeo has a neighbor who calls her dog sweetheart! She treats him like a child, or a husband; in fact, once I heard her say that he sleeps next to her, in the same bed. Isn't that the height of madness? God created dogs to guard the flocks, to protect them from wolves and keep away thieves, not to sleep in the arms of women!

Look for the truth somewhere else. I'm suspicious of that young blond guy who lived in the same apartment with the Gladiator. He has to be a spy or an agent of some secret service. I've often seen him follow me and watch me from a distance feeding the pigeons at Santa Maria Maggiore. Once he overwhelmed me with a lot of odd questions: "Why do you like pigeons so much?" "Why do you always use the elevator?" "Why are you always drinking Chianti?" "Why are you so friendly with Amedeo?" "Why do you hate pizza so much?" So I yelled right back, "What do you want from me, you spy?" Goddam spies, they're always tracking down secrets! At that moment he looked at me in surprise: "Don't you understand that I need all this information about your life for my film." Amazed, I asked, "What do you mean?" and he said, "I'm talking about the film I'm making, and you, Parviz, are going to be the star." That's when I asked myself, disconcerted, if this damn blond guy was a spy or a lunatic. When I talked to Amedeo about it, he smiled: "Parviz, don't be afraid of the blond kid, he dreams of becoming a film director someday. Human beings need dreams the way fish need water." I didn't entirely understand what Amedeo was saying, but it doesn't matter, what really counts is that I trust him completely.

I'm sure there's been a mistake. After that business of my strike against talking, Amedeo persuaded me to file an appeal, taking responsibility for the expenses. After a while they re-examined my case and admitted that I had been telling the truth, that I hadn't lied. And in the end they granted me political asylum. Besides, I'm frank and honest because I have nothing else to lose—I've already lost my children, my wife, my house, my restaurant. Let me say that I don't have much faith in the Italian police. So many times they've hauled me in to the police station to interrogate me like a dangerous criminal!

What I'm saying makes a certain amount of sense. Answer my question, please: is feeding the pigeons a crime punishable by Italian law? Now let me explain: as you know, Piazza Santa Maria Maggiore is a place where pigeons like to gather. I love the pigeons, I feel happy when I feed them. A man surrounded by pigeons is a sight that arouses the admiration of tourists, and inspires them to take souvenir pictures. And so I contribute to the promotion of tourism in Rome. But that doesn't protect me, because on more than one occasion the police have prevented me from getting near the pigeons. I've objected: "What's the law that prohibits feeding the pigeons?" I've done my best to explain that the dove is the symbol of peace in all traditions, it's even the symbol of the United Nations! I wonder how Italy can keep me from feeding the pigeons if it's a member of the UN. The police mistreated me even though I hadn't done anything serious, in fact they insulted me by saying, "You want to make beautiful Rome into a garbage dump? Go back where you came from and do whatever you want there!" I refused to give in to their threats and I kept fighting, I swore to remain faithful to the pigeons. I'll never let them die of hunger. Amedeo acted as a mediator between me and the police and they made me feed the pigeons with food provided by the city. I didn't understand the point of this agreement, but what's important is not to have any more trouble with the police and to be able to get the food without spending a cent.

But forget the abuse I get from the police. Let's talk about the concierge Benedetta, who won't stop being a bitch, just to annoy me. One time I lost patience and said to her, "It's disgraceful for a woman your age to say *guaglio'*!" but she went on repeating it shamelessly. The insults of that wretched woman have no rhyme or reason. Once she asked me, rather arrogantly, "Do you eat dogs and cats in Albania?" I kept calm, and answered her, "Do you know Omar Khayyam? Do you know Saadi? Do you know Hafiz? We are not savages who eat cats and dogs! And what the hell do I have to do with Albania!" I've been brought up since childhood to respect old people, that's why I walked away from her saying, "*Merci, Signora.*"

But let's get back to Amedeo. He's not the murderer! He can't have had anything to do with this crime. Amedeo is not stained with the Gladiator's blood. I'm sad because of his absence. I don't know exactly what's happened to him, but of one thing I'm sure: from now on no one will take any notice of me when I cry and drink wine in Piazza Santa Maria Maggiore. Who will take the bottle of Chianti away from me? I'm thinking seriously of leaving. If Amedeo doesn't come back in the next few days, I'm leaving Rome and never coming back. Ladies and gentlemen, Rome, without Amedeo, is worthless. It's like a Persian dish without the spices!

FIRST WAIL

Wednesday March 5, 10:45 P.M.

This morning Signor Benardi, the owner of the restaurant Capri in Piazza Navona, where Parviz works as an assistant cook, called me. He said Parviz doesn't do what he's told because he doesn't understand Italian, and can't distinguish between a frying pan and a saucepan, between zucchini and carrots, between basil and parsley. After a long list of complaints he offered Parviz the choice of leaving or washing dishes, and Parviz chose the second.

Thursday March 19, 11:49 P.M.

Signor Benardi called me again, telling me that he was sorry but he had to fire Parviz, because his mouth never leaves the wine bottle during working hours. He's reprimanded him many times, to no avail. Poor Parviz, he's convinced that the reason he's always getting fired is his hatred of pizza and not his poor Italian and the fact that he drinks during working hours. Now the problem is that Parviz is unemployed, so he gets even more depressed and drinks twice as much. Tomorrow, on the way home, I'll pass by Piazza Santa Maria Maggiore and find him, as usual, near the fountain, weeping and drinking. It takes a Persian meal to pull him out of that melancholy state. I'll have to remind

Stefania to invite some friends for dinner tomorrow night, so Parviz can cook his favorite dishes.

Saturday June 24, 11:57 P.M.

I've gotten fat. It seems that Parviz is right when he says, "You're a very special kind of drug addict—your drug is pizza!" I became aware of my greed for pizza only recently. There is no doubt that pizza is my favorite food, I can't do without it. By now all the symptoms of addiction are obvious. Pizza is mixed with my blood—I've become an alcoholic of pizza, rather than wine. Soon I'll soften into dough and become, in my turn, a pizza.

Thursday November 3, 10:15 P.M.

Parviz isn't wrong when he says that each of us has a place where he feels comfortable. It's enough to see him in the kitchen. He's like a king in his kingdom, finding peace and quiet in a few seconds. It seems to me that I'm seeing Shahryar, the sultan of the *Thousand and One Nights*, calm and serene after listening to one of Scheherazade's stories. The bathroom is the only place that guarantees us pure tranquility and sweet solitude; it's no coincidence that we call it the Restroom. I find tranquility in this small bathroom. It's my nest, and this white bowl where I sit to take care of my needs is my throne!

Saturday July 3, 11:04 P.M.

I've tried many times to persuade Parviz to learn the secrets of Italian cooking, but he always refuses. This subject raises many questions beyond the culinary. I think Parviz is afraid he'll forget Iranian cooking if he learns Italian. It's the only explanation for his hatred of pizza in particular and pasta in general. As the Arab proverb says: "You can't fit two swords in a single sheath." Parviz thinks it's impossible for them to live together in harmony. For him Iranian cooking, with its spices and its smells, is all that's left of his memory. Rather, it's memory and nostalgia and the smell of his family rolled into one. This cooking is the thread that ties him to Shiraz, which he has never left. Parviz is strange, he lives in Shiraz, not in Rome! So why do we force him to learn Italian and cook Italian style? Do people speak Italian in Shiraz? Do they eat pizza, spaghetti, fettuccine, lasagna, ravioli, tortellini, parmigiano in Shiraz? Auuuuuuuuu . . .

Friday April 14, 11:36 P.M.

Today I wept! I couldn't believe it, the tears flowed without my even realizing it. I never imagined finding Parviz in such a state. The social worker didn't go into details on the telephone, she said only, "Parviz is sick, hurry, before it's too late." I said to myself maybe he had drunk more than usual. I hurried to the refugee welcome center, and made my way among policemen and nurses. When I saw him with his mouth sewed up, I felt a tremendous earthquake in every part of my body. I couldn't speak, I took his hand and embraced him tightly. Oh, my God! Where does such sadness come from? What is silence? Is there any point in speaking? Are there other ways of telling the truth, without moving your lips? The authorities had told Parviz that his story of fleeing Iran was an invention, that it had nothing to do with politics, but instead with cooking! They told him, "Your application has been rejected." They didn't believe that he fled Shiraz after the Revolutionary Guard found some anti-government leaflets from the People's Mujahideen in his restaurant. It's true that Parviz is not a political activist and has no relationship to any parties, but his life was in danger. One desperate night he fled, without kissing his children or his wife goodbye; he didn't have time to say farewell to his Shiraz!

I ask as loud as I can, from this hole that has a stink to take your breath away: who possesses the truth? Rather, what is the truth? Is the truth spoken with words? Parviz spoke his truth with his mouth sewed up: he spoke with his silence.

Today my hatred of the truth has increased, and so has my passion for wailing. I'll wail for the rest of the night from this confined space, and I know that no one will hear me. To this small tape recorder I'll entrust my ceaseless wailing, then console myself by listening to it. Auuuuuuu . . .

Monday August 5, 10:49 P.M.

Peace between Parviz and the police! The controversy over the pigeons in Piazza Santa Maria Maggiore dragged on. It wasn't easy to persuade him not to feed his pigeons anymore. Parviz adores pigeons, because he's sure that someday a pigeon will land on his shoulder carrying a letter from his wife and children. He's still waiting for the promised message, especially after hearing the story of the miracle that happened in Santa Maria Maggiore in the year 356, when it snowed in August. In the meantime, the city has decided to make life difficult for the pigeons in the big squares in Rome with the excuse that there are too many of them, and they shit on the citizens and, worse, on the tourists. So it decided to prohibit feeding them in the squares. In fact, it went further, introducing free birdseed laced with birth-control chemicals. I suggested to Inspector

Bettarini that he give Parviz the job of feeding the pigeons, using the city's birdseed, and after some hesitation the police agreed. I had no trouble persuading Parviz, and obviously I said nothing to him about the nature of the city's birdseed. Sometimes it's best not to know the truth. For example, I agree with doctors who hide from a patient the true nature of his illness. What stupidity drives a doctor to say to a patient, "You're going to die in two months"? Poor man, let him live his two months without the burden of knowing the hour of his end! Is the truth a remedy that cures our ills or a poison that slowly kills us? I'll look for the answer in wailing. Auuuuuuuu . . .

Saturday February 25, 11:07 P.M.

I couldn't convince Parviz that Johan Van Marten isn't a spy but a Dutch film student who dreams of restoring the glory of neorealism with the rebirth of a De Sica or a Rossellini. Johan, or Blondie—as the residents of the building call him—is trying to gather information about the lives of Parviz, the concierge Benedetta, Sandro, Antonio Marini, Elisabetta Fabiani, Iqbal the Bangladeshi, and all the others. Johan's dream is to shoot a film in Piazza Vittorio, in black-and-white, that tells their stories. He's asked me insistently to help him persuade Parviz, Benedetta, Iqbal, Maria Cristina, and the others to be in the film. He said that Parviz is a talented actor, with remarkable artistic gifts. You merely have to watch him weeping spontaneously and feeding the pigeons near the fountain of Santa Maria Maggiore to find the many resemblances between him and the fantastic Anthony Quinn. He paused on the name. He suggested giving Parviz a name worthy of an emerging film star: Parvi Bravo instead of Parviz Mansoor Samadi.

THE TRUTH ACCORDING
TO BENEDETTA ESPOSITO

I'm from Naples, I'll shout it out, I'm not ashamed. But then why should I be? Wasn't Totò born in Naples? He's the greatest actor in the world, he won five Oscars. I'm a big fan of Totò, I haven't missed a single one of his films and I remember them all. He can make me laugh even when I'm sad. I just can't help laughing whenever I see the scene where he tries to sell the Trevi Fountain to that nitwit tourist. Remember that movie?

My name is Benedetta, but a lot of people like to call me la Napolitana. That nickname doesn't bother me. I know that a lot of the tenants can't stand me, hate me for no reason, even if I am good at my job. Ask around which is the cleanest building in Piazza Vittorio, they'll tell you with no hesitation: "Benedetta Esposito's building." I don't mean to say that I own this building, let's get it straight: I don't want any trouble with the real owner, Signor Carnevale. I'm just a simple concierge, that's all. I've spent forty years in this building, I'm the oldest concierge in Rome. I really deserve a prize, and I ought to get it right from the mayor's own hands. The problem is, this is Italy: we reward the incompetent and despise the good! Look what happened to poor Giulio Andreotti: after serving the state for decades, he was accused of being in the Mafia! Mary Mother of God, help us! In fact, they accused him of kissing that mafioso Riina on the mouth. What a disgrace! What an outrage! Who would believe such a lie? That poor man Andreotti is a true Catholic. He never misses Mass, he is a real gentleman, and as Totò says, "Gentlemen are born." I am ready to testify at the trial in Palermo loud and clear: "There is only one hand that Andreotti has kissed, and it's the hand of the Holy Father!" His back is hunched from fatigue. I have back problems, too, because of the heavy work, and the pain in my joints gives me no peace. I can't really manage the cleaning anymore, but I have no alternative since my pension isn't enough even to buy medicine. The trouble is they destroyed the Christian Democrats after Aldo Moro was killed. In the past I always voted for the Christian Democrats, but now it's all so confusing! I don't know who I should vote for. My son Gennaro told me to vote for Forza Italia, he says he heard Berlusconi on television swearing on the heads of his children he'll make everybody rich like him.

What are you saying? Signor Amedeo is a foreigner? I can't believe he's not Italian! I haven't lost my mind yet, I can certainly tell the difference between Italians and foreigners. Take that blond student, for example. There's no doubt, he's from Sweden. Just look at him and listen to him, and you know he's a foreigner, with that way he talks. He makes so many ridiculous mistakes, like when he says, over and over, "I am not *gentile*!"—"I am not polite, not nice," he says, the way someone might say, "I am *rude*." He calls me Anna Magnani! I've told him so many times that Anna Magnani was born in Rome, she's Roman, whereas I was born in Naples, I speak Neapolitan. He asked me to be in a movie. I said that I like movies a lot, especially the ones with Totò, but I don't know how to act. I'm a concierge, not an actress! At that point he took me by the hand and got me dancing. I was nearly falling down, and he looked at me seriously: "You're the new Anna Magnani!" That blond kid is a foreigner from head to toe—he's an idiot and he's crazy. A lot of times in winter I see these blond tourists, male and female, wearing short-sleeved T-shirts, and so I stop, bewildered, and in astonishment say to myself: "Aren't these people afraid of catching cold?"

But what do you want, now that I'm getting old I don't understand anything anymore. To hell with old age! And so what, if Signor Amedeo is a foreigner, as you say, then who's a real Italian? I'm not even sure about myself. Maybe the day will come when someone will say that Benedetta Esposito is Albanian or Filipino or Pakistani. Time will tell. Amedeo speaks Italian better than my son Gennaro. In fact, better than the professor at the University of Rome, Antonio Marini, who lives on the fifth floor, No. 16. I know all the tenants in my building, so they accuse me of making trouble among them. Is this the reward I deserve? I have their interests at heart and I'm always available for them. Tell me: is that supposed to mean I get involved in their business? San Genna', help me out here.

I remember very well, it was spring, five years ago. I saw him come in the street door and go toward the elevator, and I said to him:

"Hey buddy, where're you going?"

"I'm going to the third floor."

I insisted on further details, and I discovered that he was going to see Stefania Massaro. As he was about to open the elevator door I said:

"Please don't bang the door. Make sure you've closed it properly, don't press the button too hard."

He smiled at me and said:

"I've changed my mind, I'll walk."

I thought he was making a fool of me, insulting me the way everybody else does, but he smiled even more sweetly and said, "Good day, Signora!" I couldn't believe my ears! I asked myself: are there really still men who respect women in this country? That day I felt a strange sense of guilt. I swore, as sure as there's a San Gennaro, that I would be nice to him if he came back again. You should know that Signor Amedeo is the only one in this building who out of respect for me doesn't use the elevator, because he understood the problems it causes for me every time it breaks. The trials of this elevator never end. There's even someone who secretly pees in it! So I'm in danger of losing my job. We have had so many meetings to try to resolve this problem, but unfortunately we've never managed to come up with a solution. I thought of calling the people from the TV show *Striscia la notizia* who look into people's problems and solve them quickly, but then I reconsidered, I didn't want to damage the reputation of my building. Finally, inspired by James Bond, I got the idea of installing a small hidden camera in the elevator to discover the guilty party. Only I had to forget about that, because of the expense, and then I was afraid I'd be accused of spying and not minding my own business.

I was talking about Signor Amedeo, right? After a while he came to live with Stefania. I was very pleased. But this life is not fair. Tell me: does Stefania Massaro deserve a fine man like Signor Amedeo? That fart can't stand me, you'd think I'd killed her father and mother. And I can't stand her, I do my best not to run into her. How can I forget her behaviour as a child? She'd ring doorbells and make a mess on the stairs just so the other residents would get mad at me. They were always accusing me of not doing my job properly! She did everything she could to get me thrown out, but she didn't succeed. I'm not afraid of other people's spite—San Gennaro protects me, if only because I named my only son after the patron saint of Naples!

No! Amedeo has nothing to do with that crime. I don't know who killed Lorenzo Manfredini. I found him stone dead in the elevator, in a pool of blood. The people in Piazza Vittorio couldn't stand the Gladiator. I'm sure that the cause of this whole mess is unemployment. A lot of young Italians can't find a good job, so they're forced to steal for a piece of bread. The immigrant workers should be thrown out and our sons should take their places. Find the real murderer. I'm suspicious of that Albanian friend of Amedeo's. I never understood what sort of bond there was between him and Signor Amedeo. Elisabetta Fabiani informed me that she frequently saw the Albanian drunk and laughing till he cried, right in front of the tourists in Piazza Santa Maria Maggiore. I tried to warn Signor Amedeo to stay away from criminal types like that, but he wouldn't listen to me. In fact, he welcomed him into his house. And there you have the result.

I say the Albanian is the real murderer. That good-for-nothing is rude when I call him *guaglio'*! I don't know his name, and in Naples that's what we say, but he answers with a nasty word in his language. I don't remember exactly that word he always says, maybe *mersa* or *mersis*! Anyway the point is, this word means "shit" in Albanian and is used as an insult. What makes me even more suspicious is the fact that he doesn't know his own country at all. He's tried over and over again to convince me that he comes from a country that isn't Albania. He's not the only one who refuses to acknowledge his original country in order to avoid getting expelled, eh! That Filipino Maria Cristina always tells me she isn't from the Philippines, she says she's from some other country whose name I can't remember. I don't understand, why do the police tolerate these criminals? I know some of them very well, operating not far from Piazza Vittorio. You know Iqbal the Pakistani, who owns the grocery on Via La Marmora? Even he refuses to recognize his country, he always says, "I hate Pakistan." How can a person feel disgusted by his own country like that? I remember Iqbal very well. Just a few years ago, he used to unload trucks at the market in Piazza Vittorio, now he's turned into a big businessman! Tell me: how'd he find the money to start up a business? Where'd he get the money to buy the store and the van, and get the stuff that comes from outside? There's no other explanation: that bum is a thief, or a drug dealer.

So in the end what happens to the taxes we pay to the state? What's the use if not to protect us from these criminals? Why don't they arrest Iqbal and the Albanian and the rest of these criminal immigrants and throw them out? That Filipino woman, I really dislike her, she is so nasty, constantly aggravating me. My problem is I can't stand people who don't want to do anything. I still remember when she first came to take care of old Rosa, she was so thin, like a broomstick, from hunger. Oh well yes, there are still a lot of people in Africa and Brazil and other parts of the world who scrounge food out of the garbage. After a few months she got big and fat because of all the crap she eats, and she sleeps a lot, too, she only leaves the house for emergencies and pays no attention to problems like taxes, the rent, the electric bill, the phone bill, and all the other nuisances of daily life. She gets everything free and she acts like she owns the house. Is this right? Does this situation make any sense? Me, an old Italian woman, ill, I have to work hard, while she, that chubby young immigrant, is the picture of health. She eats what she wants and sleeps as much as she wants, just like a spoiled cat! I know she doesn't have papers to be here, but I can't report her because I don't want to make trouble for Rosa's relatives. They could get back at me without thinking twice.

I'm sure the murderer of Lorenzo Manfredini is one of the immigrants. The government should hurry up and do something. Soon they'll be throwing us out of our own country. All you have to do is take a walk in the afternoon in the gardens in Piazza Vittorio to see that the overwhelming majority of the people are foreigners: some come from Morocco, some from Romania, China, India, Poland, Senegal, Albania. Living with them is impossible. They have religions, habits, and traditions different from ours. In their countries they live outside or in tents, they eat with their hands, they travel on donkeys and camels and treat women like slaves. I'm not a racist, but that's the truth. Even Bruno Vespa, on TV, says so. Then why do they come to Italy? I don't know, we're full up with the unemployed. My son Gennaro doesn't have a job—if it weren't for his wife, Marina, who's a seamstress, and help from me he would have ended up as a beggar outside the church of San Domenico Maggiore in Naples. If there's no work for the people of this country, how is it that we welcome all these desperate types? Every week we see boats loaded with illegal immigrants on the TV news. They bring contagious diseases like plague and malaria! Emilio Fede always says so. But no one listens to him.

I say that crime has gone beyond all limits. Last month Elisabetta Fabiani, the widow on the second floor, lost her little dog Valentino. She had taken him out to the gardens in Piazza Vittorio to do his business, as she does every day, and she sat down to enjoy the sun, then she looked all over and there wasn't even a trace. She asked me to help, and we searched inside and outside the gardens, but not a sign. Elisabetta wept so much over the loss of Valentino that everyone thought her son Alberto had died. I told her that Valentino's disappearance raises a lot of suspicions. I don't have clear proof available, but what I see all around me tells me it was kidnapping.

First. Recently a lot of Chinese restaurants have opened in and around Piazza Vittorio.

Second. The gardens of Piazza Vittorio are the favorite place for Chinese children to play.

Third. They say that the Chinese eat cats and dogs.

After all those things I've told you, there is no doubt that the Chinese stole poor little Valentino and ate him!

Signor Amedeo is innocent. Arrest his Albanian friend, question him carefully, you'll see, he'll break down and confess. I've caught him red-handed many times trying to break the elevator. I've seen him go up and down for no reason, he goes up to the top floor and down to the ground floor. I observed him very carefully until I became sure that he was guilty. Before calling the police I spoke to Signor Amedeo to avoid complications. The Albanian is the real murderer, I'm ready to swear to it. Is it right that Signor Amedeo should pay in the place of some immigrant? Is it right to accuse a good Italian citizen of a crime he didn't commit? San Genna', you see to it!

Why are you so insistent? I told you that Amedeo is a real Italian. I asked him personally over and over to tell me where he comes from, about his parents, his family, where he was born, and other things I can't remember anymore.

He always answered with a single word: south. I didn't want to bother him with questions to find out more details, I said to myself: who knows, he might be Sicilian, Calabrian, or from Puglia. And then there's no difference between Catania and Naples, between Bari and Potenza, we all come from the south. What's the harm, in the end we're all Italians! Rome is the city where people come from all over. Do me a favor, don't accuse Amedeo of being an immigrant. We Italians are like that: in tough times we don't trust each other, instead of helping we do all we can to hurt each other. Are we a people who have betrayal in our veins? During the Second World War we fought with the Germans, then we revolted against them and were allied with the Americans. I still remember the American soldiers on the streets of Naples. I was a pretty girl then, and all the boys liked me.

We are a strange people. We murdered Mussolini and his lover Claretta in a public square in Milan, we threw out the king and his family and wouldn't let them return, we defied the Pope and the Holy Church when the majority voted in favor of divorce. Then we all saw Giulio Andreotti on television sitting at the defense table, and that no-good Cicciolina in parliament. I'm not educated like you, but I still have the right to ask: If Andreotti had dealings with the Mafia, does that mean I voted for the Mafia and didn't realize it? Does that mean that the Mafia governed Italy for decades? Lately we've been hearing about that Northern League that's doing its best to divide the country in two and found a new state, Padania. What country are we living in? Jesus, Mary, and Joseph! Madonna, help us!

I hope Signor Amedeo comes back soon. Then you will discover the terrible mistake you've made. I tell you, this country is a wonderland. From now on I won't be surprised if I hear someone say that Giulio Andreotti is Albanian or Pakistani or Filipino. Signor Amedeo is the only tenant who stops to talk to me. He always calls me Signora Benedetta and he avoids using the elevator because he respects my work, he knows how I struggle to keep things peaceful for the tenants. The disappearance of Signor Amedeo and the groundless accusation that he murdered the Gladiator make me long to leave Rome for my final return to Naples. Yes, that's San Gennaro calling me! I'll go to the church of San Domenico in Naples to pray for Signor Amedeo.

SECOND WAIL

Thursday February 4, 11:14 P.M.

I tried unsuccessfully to convince Benedetta, the concierge, that Parviz isn't Albanian, and that *merci* is a French word meaning "thank you" that is used, with the same meaning, in Iran. When I got home tonight she stopped me, as usual, and after a long tirade in which she kept repeating that I'm like her only son she advised me to stay away from the Albanian, saying, "That crook! He's just going to cause you a ton of problems, because witnesses have seen him selling drugs in Piazza Santa Maria Maggiore while he's pretending to feed the pigeons." The police have arrested him several times, but she couldn't understand why they release him right away.

Tuesday June 4, 10:57 P.M.

The morbid relationship that Benedetta has established with the elevator raises a lot of questions. This morning she was very angry with Parviz. She complained for a long time, saying that the Albanian, as she calls him, "wrecks the elevator" in order to get her fired from her job, on the pretext that she's old and can't look after the tenants. I promised to speak to Parviz to try and resolve this problem. I hate the elevator because it reminds me of a tomb. I hate confined spaces, except this bathroom. It's my nest. Today I read an article about the hoopoe in the magazine *Focus*; apparently it's the only bird that takes care of its needs in its nest! There's another bird as mysterious as the hoopoe. It's the crow, which showed Cain how to get rid of the corpse of his brother Abel by digging a pit. It's said that this was the first murder on earth, so the crow is the first expert on burial in history. I am a special sort of crow. My mission is to bury bloodstained memories.

Friday September 6, 10:35 P.M.

Our neighbor Elisabetta's dog has vanished. Tonight Benedetta asked me insistently the names of the countries where people eat dog. I answered that I don't know, then she surprised me with a strange question: "Does your friend the Albanian eat dogs and cats?" I swore that Parviz has never in his entire life touched dog or cat! This old lady has a disarming naïveté.

Wednesday November 17, 11:27 P.M.

Today Benedetta revealed a very sensitive secret to me. She said in a low voice, in order not to be heard by anyone else: "The disappearance of the dog Valentino isn't accidental. He was kidnapped by the Chinese children who play in the gardens in Piazza Vittorio! They hunt for cats and dogs the way our children chase butterflies." Then she advised me to avoid Chinese restaurants because their favorite dish is made with dog. I restrained myself from bursting into laughter, said goodbye in a hurry, and ran up the stairs. As soon as I opened the door I started laughing like a lunatic. And then I had a brilliant idea. I wondered what would happen if I knocked on Elisabetta Fabiani's door and said to her: "I've just come back from the Chinese restaurant next door, and I had rice with some delicious meat; when I was leaving I asked the restaurant owner what kind of meat I'd eaten and he said, 'It's from a dog we found one morning near our restaurant, he was wearing a collar that had "Valentino" written on it.'" I haven't laughed so much for a long time. Anyway, I hope little Valentino comes back soon, so I'll be able to listen to him wailing at night.

Saturday January 7, 11:48 P.M.

Benedetta usually complains about everything: the tenants in the building, the government, the businesses in Piazza Vittorio, how bad the health service is, the high price of medicine, taxes, rain, the immigrants. But today she talked to me about her son Gennaro, who's unemployed. She asked me to help her find him a job, repeating that when it comes to relatives, "familiarity breeds contempt," and even, "*Parenti serpenti*"—relatives are like snakes. This proverb resembles the Arab "Relatives are like scorpions." After talking about Gennaro, she began her usual complaint about the foreigners who make trouble in Piazza Vittorio and why don't the police arrest criminals like Iqbal the Pakistani who sells drugs and runs a prostitution ring. What she doesn't know or perhaps doesn't want to hear is that Iqbal is Bangladeshi, not Pakistani, and that he's not a drug pusher and has nothing to do with prostitution. Iqbal is a member of a cooperative made up of fifty Bangladeshis, and he doesn't own either the van or the shop. I've never seen anyone work like him. He's a human bee. I thought of telling Benedetta everything I know about Iqbal, then I thought twice: to what end? It's really pointless to know the truth. The only consolation is this nighttime wailing. Auuuuuuuuu . . .

Tuesday October 26, 10:53 P.M.

This morning Benedetta told me, "Today they're going to announce the final judgment on Giulio Andreotti. I don't trust informers who accuse upstanding people like Andreotti just to muddy the waters." She is waiting very anxiously for the verdict, she wants to know the truth about the relationship between the state and the Mafia. Tonight I finished reading *The Day of the Owl* by Leonardo Sciascia, which is considered one of the best novels ever written about the Mafia, and I stopped at this passage: "The truth is at the bottom of a well: look into a well and you see the sun or the moon; but throw yourself down and there is neither sun nor moon, there is the truth."

THE TRUTH ACCORDING
TO IQBAL AMIR ALLAH

Signor Amedeo is one of the few Italians who shop in my store. He's an ideal customer: he pays cash—I've never written his name in my credit book. There's a real difference between him and the rest of the customers, like the Bangladeshis, the Pakistanis, and the Indians, who pay at the end of the month. I'm well acquainted with their problems. A few can afford a fixed amount every month, while the rest live like the birds: they get their food day by day. There are a lot of Bangladeshis who sell garlic in the markets in the morning, flowers in the restaurants at night, and umbrellas on rainy days.

Signor Amedeo is different from the other Italians: he's not a fascist, I mean he's not a racist who hates foreigners, like that shit Gladiator who despises us and humiliates everyone. I'm telling you the truth: that bastard got what he deserved. The Neapolitan concierge is a racist, too, because she won't let me use the elevator when I deliver groceries to my customers who live in her building. She hates me for no reason and won't answer when I say hello. In fact, she insults me on purpose, calling me Hey Pakistani! I've told her many times, "I'm Bangladeshi, and I have nothing to do with Pakistan, in fact I have an unbounded hatred for the Pakistanis." During the war of independence in 1971, Pakistani soldiers raped many of our women. I can't forget my poor aunt, who killed herself in order not to bring shame on the family. Ah, if only we had had the bomb! I say the Pakistanis deserve to die like the Japanese in the Second World War. Not to mention the professor from Milan, who even asked me to show him authorization to use the elevator. I wondered if you need a residency permit just for the elevator.

When I see Signor Amedeo with his Iranian friend Parviz in the Bar Dandini I feel happy. I say to myself, "How nice to see a Christian and a Muslim like two brothers: there is no difference between Christ and Mohammed, between the Gospel and the Koran, between church and mosque!" Because I've been in Rome a long time I can distinguish between racists and tolerant Italians: the racists don't smile at you and don't answer if you say ciao, or good morning, or good evening. They don't give a damn about you, as if you didn't exist; in fact, they wish from the bottom of their heart that you would turn into a repulsive insect to be ruthlessly crushed. While tolerant Italians smile a lot and greet you first, like Signor Amedeo, who always surprises me with his Islamic greeting: "*Assalam alaikum.*" He knows Islam well. Once he told me that the prophet Mohammed said that "to smile at someone is like giving alms."

Signor Amedeo is the only Italian who spares me embarrassing questions about the veil, wine, pork, and so on. He must have traveled a lot in Muslim countries; maybe because his wife, Signora Stefania, has a travel agency near Via Nazionale. The Italians don't know Islam properly. They think it's a religion of bans: Drinking wine is forbidden! Sex outside marriage is forbidden! Once Sandro, the owner of the Bar Dandini, asked me:

"How many wives do you have?"

"One."

He reflected for a moment, then said:

"You're not a real Muslim, so no virgins for you in paradise, because Muslims are supposed to pray five times a day and observe Ramadan and marry four women."

I tried to explain to him that I'm poor, I'm not rich like the emirs of the Gulf, who can maintain four families at the same time, but I didn't see that he was convinced by my explanation. In the end he said to me:

"I respect you Muslim men, because you love women the way we Roman studs do, and faggots really piss you off."

And Sandro isn't the only one who says to me: "You're not a real Muslim." There's the Arab Abdu, who sells fish in Piazza Vittorio. That asshole never stops hassling me—he gets on my nerves. One moment he swears that the true Muslim has to know Arabic, the next he criticizes my last name, Amir Allah, which he considers an offense against Islam. Once he said to me:

"My name is Abdallah and you are Amir Allah. If you knew Arabic, you'd understand the difference between Abdallah, which means Slave of God, and Amir Allah, which means Prince of God."

So I told him that's my father's name and I won't ever change it, so then he called me a heretic because I consider myself a prince superior to God. This is an extremist Arab and he deserves to have his tongue cut out.

Signor Amedeo is a wanted man? I can't believe that charge. What really puzzles me is the story that all the news shows have broadcast: that Signor Amedeo is not Italian, he's an immigrant like me. I don't trust the TV reporters, because they're always looking for scandals, and they exaggerate every problem. When I hear the bad things that are said about Piazza Vittorio it makes me suspicious: I wonder if they're actually talking about the place where I've lived for ten years or the Bronx we see in cop movies.

Signor Amedeo is as good as mango juice. He helps us present our administrative appeals and gives us useful advice for dealing with all our bureaucratic problems. I still remember how he helped me solve the problem that gave me an ulcer. It began when I went to get my residency permit at the police station and realized that they had mixed up my first and last names. I explained that my first name is Iqbal and my last name is Amir Allah, which is also my father's name, because in Bangladesh the name of the son or daughter is traditionally accompanied by the father's. Unfortunately all my attempts were in vain. I went to the police station every day, until one day the inspector lost patience:

"My name is Mario Rossi, and there's no difference between Mario Rossi and Rossi Mario, just as there is none between Iqbal Amir Allah and Amir Allah Iqbal!"

Then, with the residency permit in his hand:

"This is your photograph?"

"Yes."

"This is your signature?"

"Yes."

"This is your date of birth?"

"Yes."

"Then there's no problem, right?"

"Wrong, there's a huge problem. My name is Iqbal Amir Allah, not Amir Allah Iqbal."

At that point he got angry and threatened me:

"You don't understand a goddam thing. If you come back one more time I'll seize your residency permit, take you to Fiumicino airport, and put you on the first plane to Bangladesh! I don't want to see you here one more time, get it?"

I immediately talked to Signor Amedeo about it, confessing that I was afraid of Amir Allah Iqbal and that a lot of problems could arise in the future because of this change of name. Let's say for example that someone whose name is Amir Allah Iqbal is a serious criminal or a ruthless drug dealer or a dangerous terrorist like that Pakistani Yussef Ramsi the Americans captured recently. If I adopted that new identity, how would I prove that my children are really mine? How would I prove that my wife is really mine? What would happen if they saw the marriage license and discovered that the husband of my wife is not me but another person, whose name is Iqbal Amir Allah? How would I get my money out of the bank? After my outburst Signor Amedeo promised that he would intervene to release me from this nightmare.

A few days later he kept his promise and went with me to the police station on Via Genova. It was the first time I had gone to a police station without having to wait for one or two hours. His friend, Inspector Bettarini, was expecting us, and he asked for my residency permit. Then he left the office, came back in a few minutes, and I really couldn't believe my ears when he said to me:

"Signor Iqbal Amir Allah, here is your new residency permit!"

Before thanking him I glanced quickly at the first lines of the document. Name: Iqbal. Surname: Amir Allah. I breathed a sigh of relief, truly a big weight had been lifted off my shoulders. As we were leaving the police station I had a brilliant idea: "You know, Signor Amedeo, my wife is pregnant and soon I'll be a father for the fourth time. I've decided to call my son Roberto. His name will be Roberto Iqbal!" And so it was. My wife had a boy and I called him Roberto. It's the only way for him to avoid the disaster of a mix-up between name and surname. It will be impossible to make a mistake because Roberto, Mario, Francesco, Massimo, Giulio, and Romano are all first names, not last names. I must do all I can to spare my son Roberto these serious problems. A good father should look out for his children's future.

I don't know where he is now, but I'm sure of one thing: Signor Amedeo is not an immigrant or a criminal! I'm positive he is innocent. He isn't stained with the blood of that young man who never smiled. I've known him ever since I unloaded trucks in Piazza Vittorio, before we started the cooperative. I also know his wife, Signora Stefania, she's a friend of my wife. He helped me find the house where I live, even though the owner had refused to rent to immigrants. He even persuaded me to send my wife to school to learn Italian. I really hope that Roberto turns out to be like Signor Amedeo. Now I just have to decide whether to send him to the Italian nursery school or the Islamic school, where he would learn the Koran and the Bengali language.

THIRD WAIL

T uesday February 24, 10:39 P.M.

This morning Iqbal asked me if I knew the difference between a tolerant person and a racist. I answered that a racist is in conflict with others because he doesn't believe they're on his level, while a tolerant person treats others with respect. At that point he came closer to me, and, in order not to be heard by anyone, as if he were about to reveal a secret, he whispered, "Racists don't smile!"

I thought all day about racists who refuse to smile and I realized that Iqbal has made an important discovery. The racist's problem is not with others but with himself. I would go further: he doesn't smile at his fellow-man because he doesn't know how to smile at himself. The Arab proverb that says "He who has nothing gives nothing" is very true.

Monday June 26, 10:05 P.M.

Tonight, near Piazza Venezia, I ran into Iqbal. He told me that he's suffering from an ulcer, then he looked at me sadly and said, "Amir Allah Iqbal will kill me!" His tone of voice persuaded me to take him seriously. At first I thought Amir Allah Iqbal was a person who was threatening him and wanted to kill him, and I asked him to explain, so that I could understand. We sat down in a café.

"Did you make a report to the police?"

"I've made many reports, but they threw me out."

Luckily my fears didn't last long. Iqbal pulled out his residency permit and told me the story of the mix-up of name and surname. He lingered for a long time on the problem of the similarity of names and told me a story about a man in Bangladesh who was hanged by mistake because his name corresponded exactly to that of a dangerous criminal. He looked at me, holding back tears: "You know me, Signor Amedeo, my name is Iqbal Amir Allah and I have nothing to do with Amir Allah Iqbal! You're the only Italian witness who can save me from future accusations." His words struck me. I promised that I would help him, right away. Tomorrow morning I'll call Bettarini, who was so helpful in resolving the problem of the pigeons of Piazza Santa Maria Maggiore and preventing a lot of trouble for Parviz.

Thursday January 30, 11:19 P.M.

This morning I went with Iqbal to the police station. Inspector Bettarini managed to take care of everything in a few minutes. Iqbal's joy was uncontainable. After saying goodbye to the Inspector, he insisted on inviting me to have tea in a café nearby. He's decided to name his next child Roberto, to make the job of the police easier when they have to distinguish his first and last name, and so protect his son from the same problem of the confusion of names. Iqbal is proud of the fact that his son will be the first child in the history of Bangladesh to have the name Roberto. Then he added, "I know that for you Italians our names are hard to pronounce, but this way I feel certain that all Italians will smile at my son!" I didn't want to interrupt. I let him finish and then I asked him, "What will happen if your wife has a girl?"

He reflected for a few seconds and then said, "I'll call her Roberta! Her name will be Roberta Iqbal. I swear that there is not a girl in Bangladesh who has the name Roberta." I couldn't resist the impulse to laugh. We laughed together, indifferent to the glances of the other customers. Doctors of the world unite! Invent a new remedy to cure racists of envy and hatred. Iqbal has diagnosed their illness: we need a pill like aspirin to help those wretched people smile.

Tuesday November 16, 11:39 P.M.

Tonight I went with Parviz to buy rice and spices from Iqbal. As we were talking, the subject came up of some anti-immigrant posters on the walls in Piazza Vittorio. Iqbal pointed to a box of apples in front of him: "When I see a rotten apple I immediately separate it from the rest of the apples, because if I left it there all the apples would be spoiled. Why can't the police be strict with immigrants who are criminals? Why should the honest ones who sweat for a piece of bread suffer!"

Iqbal's words opened my eyes. Labeling any immigrant a criminal, without distinction, is a déjà vu. Italian immigrants in the United States were accused of being in the Mafia, and suffered tremendously. Certainly, the Italians don't seem to have learned anything from the lessons of history.

Friday October 30, 11:04 P.M.

Today Iqbal told me with pride that his firstborn, Mahmood, speaks Italian very well. He's the one who goes with his mother on her daily rounds, to the doctor, for example, or wherever. I asked him if his wife speaks Italian, and he said that the Bangladeshis don't send their wives to school because Islam prohibits them from mixing with the opposite sex. When I got home I discussed this with Stefania, and proposed that she should organize Italian classes for Bangladeshi women. Stefania agreed, provided I could persuade Iqbal and his friends.

Tuesday March 26, 11:49 P.M.

After much hesitation Iqbal accepted the idea of an Italian class for women; his wife will attend and Stefania will teach it. I asked Iqbal to get other Bangladeshi husbands to send their wives.

Friday February 9, 11:12 P.M.

Tonight I lingered for a long time over these words from Freud's *Totem and Taboo:* "A human being's name is a principal component in his person, perhaps a piece of his soul."

THE TRUTH ACCORDING
TO ELISABETTA FABIANI

I went to a lawyer to bring suit against unknown persons. Whoever hurt little Valentino has to be punished. What Benedetta, the concierge, said about the Chinese made me suspicious. I asked the lawyer only one question: "Does the law punish people who eat dogs?" And he, taken aback, said, "I've never dealt with a question of that sort," and asked for time to consult the penal code and get advice from colleagues. I didn't sit there twiddling my thumbs. I got in touch with humanitarian groups like Amnesty International, and I have to say I was shocked. Their response was "We defend men, not animals." I say this country is not civilized. A year ago I was in Switzerland and I saw with my own eyes how dogs are treated. There are hairdressers, clinics, and restaurants exclusively for dogs. In fact, I visited a little cemetery in Geneva where man's best friends are buried. When will Italy become a civilized country like Switzerland?

Signor Amedeo is the only tolerant person in this building. He was never irritated by Valentino's barking, in fact, he was affectionate and kind to him. Stefania, his wife, hates dogs and was always complaining about Valentino. I told her that barking is the only language he has to express his joy, his sadness, his rage, and other emotions. We mustn't force him to be silent; we should be patient with him when he pees in the elevator, because he's like a child. Do we spank children when they wet their beds? We all know that dogs pee and sniff urine to communicate with the outside world. Do we want to take away their natural and legitimate rights? One time, I got fed up with Stefania's aggressiveness toward little Valentino and I yelled at her, "You're a racist, a fanatic, and I will not allow you to insult Valentino!" After that she didn't speak to me for years, whereas Signor Amedeo continued to greet me as if nothing had happened. I'm going to go to the Chinese embassy in Rome, I'll ask them to intervene. That's the only way I'll ever hold poor kidnapped Valentino in my arms again.

The Italian state should be on my side. Am I not a good citizen? Don't I pay my taxes regularly, before the deadline? Can't I claim the rights guaranteed me by the constitution? Aren't I a good Catholic who performs her religious duties properly? I've written three letters of reminder, to the Holy Father, the President of the Republic, and the Prime Minister. Each of them should carry out his proper responsibilities.

If Benedetta the Neapolitan's suspicions about the involvement of the Chinese in Valentino's kidnapping are true, then the least the Italian authorities could do to show solidarity would be to cut off diplomatic relations with China and throw the owners of Chinese restaurants in jail. No, that's nothing, they should kick China out of the U.N. and place it under embargo. No, that wouldn't satisfy me, either. Isn't it legitimate for Italy, as a member of NATO, to declare war? Aren't some of the taxes I pay deposited in NATO's coffers? Aren't there American military bases in Italian territory?

Suspicion also falls on Marina, Benedetta's daughter-in-law, who every time she saw Valentino never stopped saying, "What a sweetie! What a sweetie!" Everyone knows that Marina is Sardinian, and Sardinia is famous for kidnappings. You remember the business with Fabrizio De André and the entrepreneur Giuseppe Soffiantini? Evidently the kidnappers modified their strategy, going from men to dogs, having got the idea how much people love dogs. I'm expecting a call asking for ransom. I won't inform the police, so as not to put Valentino's life in danger. I'm ready to spend all the money I have to get Valentino back. I'm lonely without Valentino, I can't live without him.

My grand dream has been destroyed. I wanted Valentino to become a famous actor, like Inspector Rex, who tracks down criminals and arrests them. That young Dutch boy Johan asked me to be in a film he wants to make in Piazza Vittorio. I said I would accept on one condition: that Valentino should be in the film. At first he hesitated, then he said yes. I was preparing Valentino for the future, after the bashing I got from my only son. Before leaving home forever and joining those friends of his in the social-service cooperatives, Alberto said to me, "You're a jailer in this house, and I want to live without bars. This house is a market, you are a merchant, and I am a client. I want to live far away from consumer society!" I still don't understand: what do I have to do with prisons and markets? I begged him to stay, but he was indifferent to my tears. My first dream was for him to become a great movie actor like Marcello Mastroianni or Alberto Sordi, but I failed to get him into the Olympus of stars. I never give up, though; I won't accept defeat or consider something a fait accompli. That's why I decided to teach Valentino to perform difficult tricks. I went a long way with him and I was just about to reap the fruits of my hard work.

Amedeo an immigrant! How strange. Every so often we watched the demonstrations in Piazza Vittorio for the rights of immigrants: the right to work, to housing, to health care, the vote, and so on. I say that the rights of the native-born come first, and dogs are children of this country. I don't trust immigrants. I read recently in the paper that an immigrant gardener raped an old woman who had given him everything: residency permit, job, place to live, and so on. Is that the reward? Have you ever heard of a dog who raped its owner? You know the Gypsy who goes to Amedeo's house and sits with him in the Bar Dandini, and sells drugs in Piazza Santa Maria Maggiore while he's pretending to feed the pigeons? One day that scoundrel said to me:

"In my country we always leave dogs outside the house."

"What do you mean?"

"The job of a dog is to protect the house from thieves!"

"How can you say such a thing!"

I thought of reporting him for defamation and racism, then I changed my mind, out of respect for Amedeo. That stupid, criminal, racist Gypsy should be expelled from Italy immediately. The problem is that the Gypsies don't have a precise country to be sent back to!

The truth is that we don't need immigrants. I heard a politician say on TV that the Italian economy is at risk of collapsing if they stop coming. That is a lie spread by the Communists and the priests from Caritas. We can easily give up immigrants. All we have to do is teach our dogs properly— let's stop using that horrible word "train." Now, for example, there are highly educated dogs who accompany blind people when they go out to do the shopping, and who perform various other duties, just as there are dogs who help find and rescue people buried in the rubble of earthquakes. And let's not forget the dogs who work in airports, train stations, and ports whose job is to sniff out drug smugglers. We don't need immigrants. It's absurd that we teach them Italian, give them jobs and places to live, and they pay us back by selling drugs in public parks and raping our daughters. It's really too much!

Who killed poor Lorenzo Manfredini? I don't know. Ask the police. I knew the victim well. He was a friend of my son's in childhood and adolescence, they were always together, like brothers. Lorenzo came to live with his grandmother when his parents divorced, after a legal battle over the division of their assets and custody of Lorenzo. The grandmother wasn't capable of controlling her grandson, so Lorenzo left school early and has always hung around delinquents. It's very likely that he was killed by a rival gang. Like what happened in Chicago in the thirties or with the Magliana gang here in the seventies.

The government should take up the question of the cost of living right away. The solution is not to raise taxes and suffocate Italian citizens but to let dogs help: they ask nothing and perform infinite services free of charge. We have to teach them well: to arrest criminals, help old people, fix electrical appliances, prepare food, and so on. Ah, I forgot a very important thing: dogs can even work in factories without making trouble, because they don't have a union and they never go on strike. Doesn't the government want to get rid of unions? Isn't it looking for obedient workers that it can fire without legal repercussions? I believe firmly that what Professor Antonio Marini maintains is true: our big problem is underdevelopment. Unfortunately, Italy is an uncivilized country. I say that the moment has arrived to abandon dangerous ideas, such as that dogs are only good for guard duty.

Look here! There's an analogy between Amedeo's disappearance and Valentino's. I think Amedeo is the victim of a kidnapping. The police should arrest the gang of kidnappers that operates in Piazza Vittorio. Can't you see by now that there's a secret alliance between the Sardinians and the Chinese? That's the conclusion I've come to after a long investigation. I don't have enough proof, but a lot of things are suspicious, and the circumstantial evidence is very disturbing. If Valentino isn't back safe and sound in the next few days, I'm not paying taxes anymore. In fact, I'm going to emigrate to Switzerland as soon as I can and I'm never coming back to Italy.

Tuesday March 23, 10:48 P.M.
Our neighbor Elisabetta Fabiani is addicted to two things: dogs and thrillers. It's pointless to talk to her about anything in which there is no mention of a dog or of Hitchcock or Agatha Christie, Colombo or Derrick, Montalbano or Poirot. Elisabetta watches the police shows on TV every day. She is mad for the series *Rex*, which is about the adventures of a dog who is the assistant to a police inspector; he has an uncommon intelligence and performs extraordinary feats.

Saturday January 16, 11:28 P.M.
The barking of Elisabetta's dog sounds like wailing; it makes me happy. Stefania can't bear it. This morning she quarreled again with Elisabetta and threatened to call the police if her dog doesn't stop barking in the middle of the night. "You're a racist, a fanatic, you hate animals," Elisabetta accused her. Stefania was furious, and she asked me with amazement and candor, "Am I a racist and fanatic because I can't sleep at night on account of that insistent barking?" I answered, "Of course you're a fanatic, but only of love!" Then she laughed and kissed me for a long time.

Tuesday November 14, 10:57 P.M.

Tonight Elisabetta warned me about the Gypsies who sell things that have been stolen from the market in Piazza Vittorio. She told me that animals are more civilized than Gypsies from any point of view. After a long, circuitous digression she got to the point: "Don't open the door of your house to that drunken Gypsy who, under the pretext of feeding the pigeons, sells drugs." I realized that she was referring to poor Parviz. "He's not a Gypsy, he's Iranian," I reminded her, and she answered with great conviction: "It doesn't matter if he is Iranian or American or Swiss or whatever. The important thing is that he behaves exactly like a Gypsy, and that's why I say that Gypsies are not born but made." I said goodbye without commenting.

Thursday March 23, 11:45 P.M.

This morning Elisabetta asked me to support her legal battle in defense of the dogs of the world. She reported that the tenants intend to vote on a building rule that would forbid dogs to use the elevator, and that this law is directed against poor Valentino. She reminded me that racism began in the United States when blacks were forbidden to sit on buses next to whites. She would like me to sign a petition in defense of the right of Valentino and his fellow-creatures throughout the world to use the elevator, the metro, the buses, to take airplanes, trains, ships, to have the right to inherit, to sexuality, to housing, and so on. I signed the petition without discussion.

Wednesday August 27, 10:49 P.M.

This morning I ran into Elisabetta. She was very depressed. She said that she still hopes for Valentino's return, and that she possesses irrefutable proof that Sardinian kidnapping gangs are involved in what happened to her little pet. It's obvious that the dog filled her life after her husband's death and the departure of her only son. Valentino isn't simply a dog but a true companion who protects her from solitude.

Sunday October 20, 11:08 P.M.

Elisabetta's condition gets worse every day. I saw her tonight walking barefoot near Piazza Vittorio calling her vanished dog. I feel sorry for Elisabetta. How can a human being become so attached to an animal?

THE TRUTH ACCORDING
TO MARIA CRISTINA GONZALEZ

When I get married and have a child I'm going to call him Amedeo. This is a promise I've been making to myself for years. Sadly, so far I haven't experienced the joy of having children, though I've been pregnant plenty of times. I know that the Church, the Pope, and the priests are definitely against abortion, but why do they think only of the fetus? Don't I deserve a little care and attention? Who thinks about poor Maria Cristina Gonzalez?

Signor Amedeo is the only person who treats me kindly and supports me in difficult moments. I'm unfortunate and stupid, this I don't deny. My situation inspires bewilderment and surprise. Usually women are so happy when they get pregnant, but I weep, out of fear of losing my job, fear of poverty, the future, the police, everything. I sit on the stairs and cry after telling Signora Rosa the usual: "I'm going to do a little shopping." If she saw me crying she would throw me out, because she has often told me that crying brings her closer to death. And she is afraid of dying. In the beginning I used to cry alone in the bathroom. But the bathroom is horrible and sad, no one comes to rescue me. I prefer the stairs, because Amedeo doesn't use the elevator. He's the only one who asks me how I am, I tell him my troubles and cry on his shoulder.

Signora Rosa is eighty. She was paralyzed ten years ago, and she only leaves her wheelchair to go to the bathroom or to lie down in her bed. She has four children, who take turns coming to see her every Sunday for a few hours. When one of them arrives, my weekly holiday begins: from noon to midnight! I don't know what to do to enjoy my brief time off. I look at the hands of the clock on the wall and hope from the bottom of my heart that time will stop, so my freedom will last longer. I do all I can not to waste precious minutes, I make a plan filled with activities, but in the end I do the same thing every time: I go to the station where the Peruvian immigrants gather. Their faces satisfy my thirsting eyes and their words warm my cold ears. It seems to me I've gone home, to Lima. I greet them all with a kiss even if I've never seen them before, then I sit on the sidewalk and eat Peruvian food, rice with chicken and *lomo saltado* and ceviche. I talk for hours, I talk more than I listen, that's why they call me Maria Cristina the chatterbox.

When the sun begins to set, I get more and more depressed, knowing that my journey to freedom is about to end. So I cling to the bottles of beer and Pisco to shelter myself from that storm of sadness. I drink a lot to forget the world, to forget my problems. I'm not the only one who has to deal with old age and imminent death every day. There are a lot of us, united by the destiny of our work with old people who at any moment will move on to another world. As the time passes we are transformed into stray dogs. Some let their tongues go, hurling insults in Spanish and Italian. Some provoke the people sitting nearby, and so in an instant fists are raised, and kicks and punches fly. I, instead, move silently out of sight, and under the wing of night go with a young man who resembles me in every way. Each of us empties into the other's body our own desire, hope, anguish, fear, sadness, rage, hatred, and disappointment, and we do this quickly, like animals afraid of missing the season of fertility. We lie on an isolated bench or on pages of a newspaper spread out on the ground. Lots of times I forget the pill and here begins my pregnancy problem, the mad attempt to abort. I know that the pill is very important, but I always forget because I've had so much to drink.

I often wish old Rosa would die. Yet when I think of the consequences I'm filled with a strong feeling of regret—I'm afraid that her death also means the end of me. Where can I go? How can I support my family in Lima? What will become of me? This life is just not fair. Must I live out my youth a prisoner among phantoms of death? I want a house, a husband, children. I imagine waking in the morning, taking my children to school, going to work, embracing my husband at night, and finally seeing our bodies join on a comfortable bed and not on a sad park bench or an abandoned train car or under a hidden tree.

I would like to feel at peace but I don't even have documents. I'm like a boat with torn sails, subject to the will of reefs and waves. If I had a residency permit I wouldn't let that Neapolitan concierge make fun of me and insult me. She always calls me the Filipino. I've told her many times, "I'm not from the Philippines, I'm from Peru!" I'm from Lima, I don't understand how someone can confuse Peru with the Philippines! I don't even know why she persists in insulting me. One day I lost patience and said to her, "Why do you despise me? Have I somehow been disrespectful to you without realizing it?" For example, I know she's from Naples but I've never insulted her by calling her la Napolitana. So many times I've said to her, "Why are you so rude to me, don't you see that we belong to the same religion, that love for the Cross and the Virgin Mary unites us?"

I'm afraid of the concierge because she could report me to the police. I don't have a residency permit, and if I fell into their hands they wouldn't be indulgent with me and in the blink of an eye I would find myself back in the airport in Lima, back in the inferno of poverty. I don't want to return to Peru before achieving my dream of a house, a husband, and children. When I have a residency permit I won't be afraid to say whatever I want, I won't call her Signora Benedetta, I'll say "Neapolitan concierge"! I pray to the Virgin Mary, only she will save me from these cruel people.

I suffer terribly from loneliness, and sometimes it makes me caress madness. I watch TV all day and eat, I devour huge quantities of chocolate. As you see, I'm very fat. I'd like to lose weight, but in these conditions I can't manage it. It's not a big deal, losing weight isn't so hard. When I get married I'll feel calmer and then my weight will go down automatically. They wouldn't let me have my friends in the house after the neighbors complained. The truth is that that damn Benedetta said bad things about me to the old lady's daughter, Signora Paola, telling her that I bring men home and stay with them all night, so then I don't take care of the sick woman. Then they said my weight was responsible for breaking the elevator, they say it's more than the capacity of the poor elevator. They said to me, "First lose weight, then use the elevator!"

Is it right that they forbid me to use the elevator while they let Signora Fabiani's dog pee there? That dog is happier than I am, he goes out more than ten times a day, he wanders in the gardens in Piazza Vittorio like a little prince or a spoiled child. Instead I can't leave the house even for a minute, because Signora Rosa has heart problems. What would happen if her heart stopped beating while I'm not there? I don't want to think about the consequences. I envy little Valentino. I've often dreamed of being in his place. Am I a human being? Sometimes I doubt my humanity. I don't even have time to go to Mass on Sunday or put myself in the hands of a priest to confess and wipe away my sins. So I'll be damned, and Hell will be waiting for me in the next world.

Signor Amedeo a murderer! That's ridiculous. I'm sure he's innocent. And they accuse him of being an immigrant. Is immigration a crime? I don't understand why they hate us so much. Fujimori, the ex-President of Peru, was an immigrant from Japan. You hear so many lies about immigrants on TV. And yet in spite of that I can't do without television. Once the TV broke. My hands shook, my heart was pounding. I called the four children of Signora Rosa one after another and asked them to come right away. They thought their mother was dead or about to die, Signor Carlo even called a funeral home before he came, and when they arrived they found a depressing situation. Signora Rosa was there yelling at me to stop crying. I gathered my strength and said to them, "I will not remain in this house a moment longer if you don't get the TV fixed immediately." Signora Laura asked her husband to get a new television. The four children of Signora Rosa left the house when, reassured, they saw me watching a new episode of *The Bold and the Beautiful* on channel 5. TV is a friend, a brother, a husband, a child, a mother, and the Virgin Mary. Can one live without breathing?

I watch the Mexican and Brazilian telenovelas every day, and I know all the details of the actors' lives. It's enough to tell you that the last episode I saw upset me as if it were my own mother's funeral. Anyway, I don't consider myself simply a spectator but an actress who plays an important role in the serial. I often shout advice at the characters. "Marina, watch out, Alejandro doesn't love you, he's a cheat, he wants to get your money and throw you out of your father's castle," or "Talk to her, Pablo, tell her you love her and want to marry her!" or "Caterina, don't be hard on your husband, you'll drive him into the arms of his new lover, that whore Silvana!" Often I feel solidarity with the poor, the unfortunate and despised. I get up from my chair, go to the TV, stare the bad man or woman in the eye: "What do you think, you rat, you'll get what you deserve, the good will win in the end!" or "Carolina, you are vile, why are you so mean to Eleonora, that poor orphan? Damn you, you deserve to go to hell," or "Julio, you'll never find peace, you're a criminal and you'll get your punishment—that young, good-looking Alfonso Rodriguez will see to it!"

Yesterday on RAI 3 I saw a program about infertility, and I learned that the main cause of it is anxiety. I said to myself, for consolation, that abortion has at least one positive aspect—it proves that I'm healthy. And this means, fortunately, that I can hope to have children and a husband and a house, and weigh the same as Claudia Schiffer, Eva Herzigova, Naomi Campbell, Laetitia Casta, and the wife of Richard Gere, whose name I can't remember. It's possible that I'll become a famous actress in the near future, especially after that young Dutch Johan insisted on having me in his next film. I told him I don't have a residency permit, but that didn't matter to him. I asked him to give me some time to lose weight, but he got angry: "I hate Hollywood cinema because it betrays reality. Don't lose weight. Being fat makes you more beautiful." After calming down he apologized: "I'm against any form of catenaccio." I didn't understand what he meant and I wondered: "What is catenaccio?" I heard some tenants say that Johan is nuts. It doesn't matter, I wouldn't marry him, have children by him. What matters to me really is to become a famous actress. Then who will dare prevent Signora Maria Cristina Gonzalez, thin, beautiful, the mother of Amedeo, Jr., from using the elevator?

S aturday May 23, 10:55 P.M.
Today I read an article in the *Corriere della Sera* with a significant title: "Is the Italian a Dinosaur?" The article analyzes the problem of Italy's falling birth rate; compared with the other countries of the world its growth rate is very low. The author states that the Italian is doomed to die out in the next century. The solution lies in the increasing presence of immigrants. Maybe Italy should make an agreement with the Chinese authorities to import human beings. There really are a lot of old people in this country.

Sunday October 26, 11:29 P.M.
This afternoon I saw Maria Cristina at the station with her fellow-countrymen and she seemed happy, like a fish returning to the sea after a brief agony far from the water. You can't help feeling sorry for that girl; she goes out of the house only for a few minutes at a time to do the shopping. Maria Cristina suffers terribly from solitude within those four walls.

Wednesday June 23, 9:58 P.M.
Tonight I saw a great film on TV, with Alberto Sordi and Claudia Cardinale, which tells the story of a certain Amedeo, an immigrant who works in Australia. The life of

Italian immigrants in the past closely resembles the life of the immigrants arriving in Italy today. Throughout history, immigrants have always been the same. All that changes is their language, their religion, and the color of their skin.

Tuesday October 26, 11:44 P.M.

Tomorrow Maria Cristina will go to the doctor for an abortion, not for the first time. Stefania is right when she says that Maria Cristina will enter the *Guinness Book of Records* for the number of abortions she's had. I wonder if I'm like her, if all I do is abort. Is wailing an abortion of the truth? Auuuuuuuuuu . . .

Thursday June 3, 10:09 P.M.

This morning I read an article by the philosopher Karl Popper on the influence of television in our daily lives. Popper maintains that TV has become a member of the family, and that its voice is the most listened to in the whole family. Maria Cristina said to me one day, "TV is my new family."

Saturday April 20, 11:52 P.M.

Tonight I quarreled with Lorenzo Manfredini. I told him to leave Maria Cristina alone. That poor girl lives in a prison. I thought of going to Inspector Bettarini, but I was afraid of causing problems for her, because she doesn't have a residency permit. That thug doesn't deserve his nickname, the Gladiator. It's an insult to Spartacus, the liberator of the slaves!

THE TRUTH ACCORDING
TO ANTONIO MARINI

This morning I waited half an hour for the 70 bus at the terminus on Via Giolitti, near Piazza Vittorio. Finally three buses arrived, one after the other. The drivers got out, paying no attention to the people waiting, went over to the café across from the bus stop, and sat down at a table outside to drink coffee, smoke cigarettes, and chat. We waited another half hour to leave. Eventually, the drivers got up, climbed into their buses, and drove off! Madonna! Where in the world are we? In Mogadishu or Addis Ababa? In Rome or Bombay? In the developed world or the Third World? Pretty soon they'll throw us out of the club of rich nations. These things don't happen in the north. I'm from Milan and I'm not used to this chaos. In Milan keeping an appointment is sacred—no one would dare say to you, "Let's meet between five and six," which in Rome happens frequently. In such cases my policy is to say firmly, "We'll meet at exactly five or at exactly six!" What's the meaning of the expression "Time is money" if no one takes account of it? The decision to leave Milan and come to Rome wasn't a wise one. I gave in to pressure from my father: "Antonio, go to Rome, don't lose the chance to work when you have it, son! Work is precious." So I accepted the job of assistant professor in the department of modern history at the Sapienza University of Rome. At first I had thought I would stay a year or two at most and then return to Milan, but I resigned myself to the situation when I got a professorship. Now I'm about to retire. How I regret all the years I've spent here!

Rome! The eternal city! Beautiful Rome! Beloved Rome! No, I'm sorry, I don't look at Rome with the eyes of the visitor who comes for a week or two, tours Piazza Navona, Piazza di Spagna, the Trevi Fountain, takes some souvenir photos, eats pizza and spaghetti, and goes back to his own country. I don't live in the paradise of tourists; I live in the inferno of chaos! For me there is no difference between Rome and the cities of the south, Naples, Palermo, Bari, and Siracusa. Rome is a city of the south; it has nothing to do with cities like Milan, Turin, and Florence. The people of Rome are lazy, that's the obvious truth. They live off the fat of the land, exploiting the ruins, the churches, the museums, and that sun which all the tourists from northern Europe are mad about. Imagine Rome without the Coliseum, St. Peter's dome, the Trevi Fountain, and the Vatican Museums! Laziness is the daily bread of the Romans. Just listen to the dialect they use in conversation: they swallow half their words out of laziness. I get angry when my Roman colleagues at the university call me Anto', and I say to them, with annoyance, "My name is Antonio!" You just have to watch the films of Alberto Sordi, like *Count Max* or *Il Marchese del Grillo* or *A Very Little Man*, to discover the truth about the Romans. They're proud of their failings; they aren't embarrassed to express their admiration for the woman who betrays her husband or the person who doesn't pay taxes or the delinquent who rides the bus without a ticket! I hate their arrogance. Remember Alberto Sordi's line "I am me, and the rest of you are less than shit"? That is the true nature of the Romans.

Isn't the wolf, after all, the symbol of Rome? I never trust the children of the wolf, because they're wild animals. Cunning is their greatest talent for taking advantage of the sweat of others. So the people of the north work, produce, pay taxes, and the people of the south use this wealth to set up criminal organizations like the Mafia, the Camorra, the *'ndrangheta*, and the gangs of kidnappers in Sardinia. The tragedy is that the north is an economic giant and a political dwarf. That's the bitter truth. I always advise my students to read *Christ Stopped at Eboli*, that wonderful book by Carlo Levi, to understand how the south was born into laziness and underdevelopment. Nor has the situation changed compared with the past; the mentality has stayed the same. There's no point in racing ahead of ourselves, the time has come to admit that the unification of Italy was an irreparable historical mistake.

Amedeo is an immigrant! To me there is no difference between immigrants and people from the south. Even though I don't understand Amedeo's relationship to the south. I'm an attentive observer, I can distinguish between someone who is lazy and someone who wants to work. For example, the Neapolitan concierge, Sandro Dandini, and Elisabetta Fabiani are symbols of the south, with their sadness, their chatter, their underdevelopment, gossip, credulousness, superstition. I'm not a racist. I can quote the great Neapolitan historian Giustino Fortunato, patented southerner, who maintains that the tragedy of the south is the uncertainty of tomorrow. They do not plant and they do not sow, that is, they do not invest. The early bird catches the worm.

When the concierge told me that Amedeo is from the south I didn't believe it, because his way of speaking, of greeting, of walking resembles that of the Lombards, the Piedmontese. I didn't ask where he was from. Such things have to do with his private life, and I have no right to meddle. Once I heard him say, "I'm from the south of the south." So I deduced that Rome is the south and the cities of southern Italy like Naples, Potenza, Bari, and Palermo are the extreme of the south! We ran into each other often in the history department library at the university. We touched on various subjects regarding the history of ancient Rome, and I discovered that he was very well versed in Roman colonialism in Africa. I saw him reading Sallust's *War of Jugurtha*. What caught my attention was his knowledge of St. Augustine. He is obviously a true Catholic. He believes in the values of the Church, in the sacredness of work and family. He also knows the Bible. I recall a long discussion we had of Jesus' saying "If you continue in my word, then are you my disciples indeed; and you shall know the truth, and the truth shall make you free." He wasn't convinced that the truth will make us free. In fact, on the contrary, the truth according to him is a chain that makes us slaves. I know that he is a translator, but I didn't ask him what language he translates from. I can't believe that he is the murderer.

A sense of outrage keeps me from remaining silent: do you know that the residents of our building pee in the elevator? It's really disgraceful. Certainly Amedeo is not among the suspects, because he never uses the elevator—he prefers the stairs. I've frequently advised him not to take the stairs: going up and down all the time can cause a heart attack, according to a study by researchers at the Pasteur Institute. But he paid no attention. I've tried quite a few times to organize tenants' meetings to deal once and for all with some serious problems, especially the problem of the elevator. I repeated that the elevator is a matter of civilization, and that we must establish clear rules for using it: tossing out cigarette butts is prohibited, eating is forbidden, writing obscenities is prohibited, urinating is forbidden, and so on. I proposed putting a sign on the door of the elevator: "Please keep the elevator clean!" But the proposal did not win a majority vote, and afterward the Dutch student Van Marten went off saying, "Such a sign should only be at the entrance to a public toilet!"

The breakdown of the elevator is a catastrophe that forces us to use the stairs, and is thus an offense to modernity, to development, and to enlightenment! I've often tried to convince the other residents, but without success. I said, "The elevator is a means of transport produced by civilization. It saves time and effort, it's as important as the train or the airplane." I categorically refuse to walk, to waste time by going up and down the stairs. I read a book recently by an American sociologist who claims that the authorities in Los Angeles decided to eliminate pedestrian crossings because people don't walk anymore. I wonder: when will we get rid of stairs in Italy?

Amedeo is a contradictory person: he goes to libraries for research and study, yet he spends hours at Sandro's. This habit is typical of people from the south: sitting in a café talking and gossiping. We should close down the cafés and force everyone to work. Amedeo was not lucky; if he had lived in Milan he would have had a different fate. Unfortunately, going to Sandro's has had a negative influence on his way of life. As we in Milan say, "Worse than a Roman." Even the Dutch student Van Marten has not been safe from the negative cultural and social influences of the Romans.

I've often heard him say, with arrogance and no shame, "I am not *gentile*!" At first I ignored it because he is a foreigner and hasn't mastered Italian properly. I tried to correct this error; I am, first of all, a teacher. I took him aside in order not to offend him, saying to him in a low voice, "Don't repeat that phrase, because, in a word, it means that you are uncivilized and have no manners; that is, that you are a barbarian." He looked at me with an air of false innocence: "I know that the word '*gentile*' means well brought up, kind, and polite, but I mean something else." I couldn't listen to the rest of his explanation because my role as a respectable university professor prevents me from engaging with a foreign student who intends to debate me on a matter having to do with the Italian language!

I say that this country is drowning in the sea of miracles. The soccer world championships, for example, demonstrate how the Italians discover they are Italians: they hang national flags in the window, on balconies, in stores. How marvelous, soccer creates identity! Is it really useful to have a single language, a common history, a common future? What is the point of Italian unity? Where are we? Is this how things work in an underdeveloped country? God damn!

I have to admit that Amedeo's giving up the use of the elevator, the bus, and the metro and his passion for walking for hours led me to believe that he belonged to a political movement much more dangerous than Nazism, Fascism, or Stalinism. I'm talking about those lousy Greens! I have no problem calling the supporters of the environment new barbarians, because they do their utmost to stop the train of development and technology and carry humanity back to prehistory with ridiculous messages like saving the trees, closing the big factories, forbidding hunting, and boycotting the products of Nestlé and McDonald's. I know the history of these new barbarians—am I not a historian? These people represent the continuation of the student revolution of '68 that failed miserably. Poor devils, they thought they would change the world with Chairman Mao's Little Red Book and the anti-technology works of Herbert Marcuse. Many of these failures have gained power by riding the wave of defending the environment. The proof is the former leader of the French students, Daniel Cohn-Bendit, who got a seat in the European Parliament. And let's not forget that the Greens are part of the government in Germany! I posed a single question to Amedeo and begged him to answer yes or no:

"Are you an activist for the Greens?"

He answered without hesitation: "No."

I drew a sigh of relief and opened the door of the elevator, cursing the barbarians, ancient, modern, and postmodern.

Don't ask me who the murderer is, I am a university professor, not Lieutenant Columbo. By the way, do you know what the young man found murdered in the elevator was called? The Gladiator. That is sufficient to demonstrate the backwardness of the Romans and their pathological attachment to the past. You would never find a person in Milan who would give himself a name like that. Such things happen only in the south.

SIXTH WAIL

Tuesday December 4, 11:08 P.M.

I went with Stefania to the Tibur theater in San Lorenzo. We saw Gianni Amelio's *The Way We Laughed*. It won the Golden Lion in Venice, and tells the story of Italian emigrants who left the cities and towns of the south after the war and moved to the north to work for their daily bread in the hope of a better future. The workers of the south deserve the credit for the industrial rebirth of the north and the flowering of the Fiat factories. I don't understand why Antonio Marini accuses the people of the south of laziness and lack of faith in tomorrow!

Friday June 4, 10:50 P.M.

Today I ran into Antonio Marini in the Sapienza library. We talked for a long time about the Roman Empire and discussed questions of colonialism in general. I told him that in my opinion the peoples who have endured colonialism in the course of history bear a substantial share of the responsibility. I reflected on the Algerian intellectual Malek Bennabi's concept of "colonizability." This colonizability—that is, a susceptibility to colonialism—is the result of a betrayal among brothers. May Bocchus, the betrayer of Jugurtha, who was sold to the Romans, and his followers be damned forever. Auuuuu . . .

Thursday November 15, 10:48 P.M.

Marini complains a lot about the bus drivers. He says they don't do their job properly and should be sent to Milan to learn from their colleagues. He always says that the unification of Italy was a crime against the north and that the south is a heavy burden for the people of the north. If I were a Buddhist I would say that this man was reincarnated as the neighborhood rooster because he sings so much, maybe too much!

Monday April 9, 11:23 P.M.

Stefania is right when she calls Antonio Marini the traffic cop. Luckily I don't use the elevator, so I can keep clear of his obsession. This man has been stricken by a new malady, "elevator-mania," very similar to paranoia. He never stops repeating that the elevator is civilization and that the fundamental difference between the civilized and the barbarians lies, first of all, in safeguarding the elevator.

Saturday August 12, 10:54 P.M.

Tonight Marini advised me to use the elevator, and told me that going up and down the stairs can cause a heart attack or a broken femur and other physical problems. He asked me to come to the next meeting where the elevator will be discussed. Taking my hand and looking me in the eye he said to me, "I know that you are the only civilized person in this building. Help me in the battle against the new barbarians." I promised him that I would try to convince the other tenants how important it is to take care of the elevator.

Thursday March 23, 11:49 P.M.

This morning Marini asked me insistently if I'm a supporter of the Greens, since I never take the elevator or the bus and always prefer to walk. I said no, and I saw him draw a sigh of relief. According to him the supporters of the environment are the new barbarians and the mortal enemies of civilization, because they would like to stop progress and scientific research, and thus return humanity to its prehistory. He concluded his lesson with a warning: "Watch out for the Greens. They are more dangerous than the Nazis, the Fascists, the Red Brigades, the Stalinists, and the Khmer Rouge."

Monday March 2, 10:47 P.M.

This morning as usual I read Montanelli's column in the *Corriere della Sera*. He raised a question very dear to the Northern League, the question of secession. Writing with his usual frankness, he said that the crux of the problem consists in the fact that Italy was born before the Italians; that explains the fragility of Italian unity, which was imposed by a minority despite rejection by the majority. Montanelli's words led me to think seriously about all this talk that aims at the integration of immigrants into Italian society. I wonder if there is an Italian society that truly accepts the idea of integration for immigrants. At the moment I couldn't care less about integration. What I really care about is how to be suckled by the wolf without her biting me, and to enjoy my favorite game: wailing! Auuuuuu . . .

The Truth According to Johan Van Marten

M y father wasn't very enthusiastic about my project and tried every means to get me to reconsider my decision: "Johan, forget Italy, you won't learn anything from the Italians. Remember, that's the country that invented catenaccio! That system of defensive lockdown would have killed the game, if the Dutch hadn't invented total soccer." I still remember his parting words to me at the airport. "Remember, Johan, Milan became one of the best teams in Europe—and the world—thanks to the Dutch trio of Gullit, Van Basten, and Rijkaard, not Berlusconi's money." My father never forgave my disobedience and so he started teasing me, calling me Gentile, because in his opinion I don't deserve the name Johan, which reminds him of the great player Cruyff.

I know that "gentile" is an Italian word that means polite and well mannered, but actually it's the surname of the former player for Juventus and for the Italian national team that won the world championship in 1982 in Spain, who today is the coach of the national under-21 team. Claudio Gentile was known for his aggressiveness and for man-to-man marking. For my father Gentile is the primary enemy of the sport, in fact the ultimate symbol of catenaccio. In his opinion the international soccer federation should have disqualified him when he made Maradona cry and ripped Zico's shirt at the world championship in Spain. That's why I keep saying "I am not GENTILE"—it's my way of saying I'm innocent. But is Gentile the true image of Italy?

I came to Rome to study film and realize the dream I've had since I was a child. I love Italian films; my true passion is neorealism, which in my view is the best response there's been to Hollywood. I adore the films of Rossellini and De Sica. Rossellini's *Rome Open City* and De Sica's *Bicycle Thief* are among the finest films in the history of cinema. Some scenes from *The Bicycle Thief* were shot right here in Piazza Vittorio. That's what inspired me to rent a room in the building where Amedeo lives in Piazza Vittorio.

Of course I still remember our first meeting. I saw him come out the street door of the building with the film *Divorce Italian Style* under his arm, I asked him the name of the director and he said, "Pietro Germi. This film is the masterpiece of Italian cinema." I told him that I preferred the neorealist films and at that point he looked at me with a smile: "This subject deserves a cineaste's dissertation at Sandro's bar." That day we had a conversation about the state of Italian cinema, and how it's become a victim of bureaucratic obstructionism. Amedeo maintained that Italian-style comedy represents the highest level of Italian creativity because it emphasizes paradoxes, combines tragedy and comedy, humor and serious criticism. So I realized that Amedeo is an open person and not a supporter of catenaccio.

No, no. Catenaccio really does have to do with this! It's not just a defensive tactic in soccer but a way of thinking and living, a result of underdevelopment, of locking the chain and throwing away the key. There are plenty of examples of the culture of catenaccio in Rome. To mention one, after the New Year holidays last year, when I came back from Amsterdam I decided to bring gifts for some Italian friends. The police stopped me and brought me to headquarters to question me. I didn't understand why, I thought it was a mistake. They searched my suitcase, found a few grams of marijuana, and said to me:

"What's this?"

"Presents for my friends."

"Are you making fun of us, you son of a bitch?"

"No. I'm telling you the truth, it's not against the law."

"Are you crazy?"

"These are presents for friends, here's the receipt from the store in Amsterdam."

"Are you Dutch?"

"Yes."

"Ah, that explains everything."

"I don't understand."

"Rome is not a paradise for drug addicts, like Amsterdam! Selling drugs is illegal in Italy. Now do you understand? Possession of marijuana is a crime punishable by the law."

In the end they let me go, after making me swear that I wouldn't bring drugs into Italy and that I would give up marijuana for good. I still don't understand what marijuana has to do with drugs like heroin. Isn't there a European Union? Doesn't the freedom to smoke, believe, and think exist in Italy? Is Italy a civilized country? My troubles with the police are not confined to this one incident. One night I went to Via Gioberti, near the station, where the prostitutes are, and there was an African girl I liked; we agreed to go to her room in a hotel nearby. I was just heading over there when the police stopped me and assaulted me with questions. At a certain point I couldn't take it anymore: "I don't understand why you're arresting me. You don't have the right. I made an arrangement with her, I've already given her the money, I haven't committed any crime. And then isn't this the red-light district, like the one in Amsterdam?" I nearly spent the night in jail.

Amedeo is a foreigner! Is it logical that the person who represents magnificent Italy is a foreigner? He's the only one who answers all my questions about politics, the Mafia, movies, cooking, and so on. Also, I don't understand why Amedeo has been accused of murdering the Gladiator. I know Lorenzo Manfredini very well—I shared an apartment with him. He adored dogs. Just have a look around his apartment and you'll see hundreds of photographs of dogs on the walls. Someone who loves dogs the way he did doesn't deserve to die like a criminal. I know that he wasn't liked by the other tenants because of his strange behavior. He always said to me, "I'm a stray dog and I have no master."

Did Amedeo harbor some anger toward Lorenzo? I don't know. I'm sure that finding the body in the elevator has a precise meaning. Most of the fights between the tenants originate with the elevator. All the meetings focus on it: Mr. Elevator! Once I lost my temper and shouted, "Do you realize that the Dutch parliament recently approved a law that allows an individual to kill himself? It's the first law in the world that legalizes euthanasia. While the Dutch people passionately debate this new law, we are discussing the use of the elevator!" This is underdevelopment, this is fucking catenaccio! I left the meeting in a fury. The elevator is the source of the problem. There is no agreement among the tenants about it: there are some who want air-conditioning in summer and heat in winter, there are some who propose putting a crucifix and photos of the Pope and Padre Pio in it, while some insist on the right to a secular elevator with no religious symbols. Then, there are some who reject all these proposals, maintaining that they are costly and unnecessary. In other words, this elevator is like a ship with more than one captain.

Slowly I began to get to know the tenants, thanks to the methods of neorealism, and I discovered that the elevator would be a good subject for a film that combines neorealism and the cinema of Fassbinder. Some splendid titles came to mind: *Catenaccio*, or *Mr. Elevator* or *The Elevator of Piazza Vittorio*, or *Clash of Civilizations Italian Style* or *Clash of Civilizations Over an Elevator in Piazza Vittorio*. I dreamed of giving the role of the protagonist to Hanna Schygulla, who was in Fassbinder's big films. The role of the owner of the dog who disappeared could be right for her. I'm a great admirer of the Iranian Parviz because he reminds me of Anthony Quinn in his early films. And the Neapolitan concierge Benedetta also has an important role, because she represents the character of the people, like Anna Magnani in *Campo de' fiori*. I asked Amedeo to help me persuade all the people in the building to be in the film. I'm enthusiastic about making this film, and even more so after the murder. That's already publicity. I'm not turning back—I'm going to continue on my path.

SEVENTH WAIL

Saturday November 7, 11:43 P.M.

Today I met a young Dutch fellow called Johan. He's a film student who's a fan of neorealism. We had a long discussion about reality in Italian movies, and I strongly defended Italian comedy, which often takes on serious and sad subjects in a comic manner. I love Pietro Germi's film *Divorce Italian Style*, I'm never bored, no matter how often I see it. It's the story of a man who devises a plan to kill his wife so that he can marry a young woman. It's said that this film prepared the way for the referendum on divorce in Italy in 1974.

Friday March 25, 11:55 P.M.

I went to the Mamertine prison near the Coliseum for the first time: it was a moving experience. There, in 104 BC, our great warrior Jugurtha died, after six days without food or water. Goddam traitors. On the way home I met the Dutch student, and talked to him for a long time about Jugurtha and his struggle against the Romans. He said to me, "You're the only Italian who knows the history of Rome. The story of that African hero would be a great subject for an epic like Stanley Kubrick's *Spartacus*."

Wednesday May 25, 10:53 P.M.

Johan asked me to be his guide to Rome. Tomorrow we're going to Campo de' Fiori, where the famous film with Anna Magnani and Aldo Fabrizi was shot. In the middle of this square Giordano Bruno was burned at the stake. Now in this cursed place there's a big statue in memory of the philosopher.

Saturday November 30, 22:39 P.M.

Tonight I went with Johan to the Goethe Institute to a retrospective devoted to the German director Werner Rainer Fassbinder. We saw *Ali: Fear Eats the Soul.* It's the story of a Moroccan immigrant, al Hadi, who is called Ali, and his wife, a German woman the age of his mother. The two are under constant pressure because of the hostility and arrogance of the people around them: neighbors, colleagues at work, and especially the woman's family. Fassbinder describes the tragedy of Ali, torn between his nostalgia for couscous and his desperate attempts to please the Germans.

Monday April 20, 11:35 P.M.

I ran into Johan tonight. He was rather depressed because of the bureaucratic obstacles that keep him from making *Clash of Civilizations Over an Elevator in Piazza Vittorio*, but although he was complaining about what he defines as the "catenaccio mentality," Johan hasn't lost his enthusiasm. "The film will be very successful," he told me. "I'll use a theater setup, with a single background—that is, the entrance to the building facing the elevator. I'll persuade the tenants to play their roles the way people did in the era of neorealism: Benedetta will become a famous actress like Anna Magnani!"

*

Friday November 30, 11:16 P.M.

Blond Johan has decided to go ahead with his film about the tenants' morbid relationship with the elevator. I asked him to leave me out, simply because I don't use the elevator. All my nightmares take place in an elevator: a narrow tomb without windows.

THE TRUTH ACCORDING
TO SANDRO DANDINI

I'm the owner of the Bar Dandini, which looks out on the gardens of Piazza Vittorio. Most of my customers are foreigners. I know them well, and I can tell the difference between a Bangladeshi and an Indian, between an Albanian and a Pole, between a Tunisian and an Egyptian. The Chinese, for example, pronounce the letter *l* in place of *r*, as in "Good molning, olange juice." The Egyptians say *b* instead of *p*, for example, "A cabbuccino, blease." As you see, it won't be easy to convince me that my friend Amede' isn't Italian.

Amede' is Amedeo. In Rome we're in the habit of eliminating the first letters or the middle or final ones of a name; for instance, I'm called Sandro but my real name is Alessandro, my sister's name is Giuseppina but we call her Giusy, everyone calls my nephew Giovanni Gianni, my son is Filippo but we always call him Pippo, and there are plenty of other examples.

I met Amedeo when he came to live in Piazza Vittorio. I still remember our first encounter: he asked for a cappuccino and a *cornetto*, and then he sat down and began reading Montanelli's column in the *Corriere della Sera*. I've never in my life seen a Chinese, a Moroccan, a Romanian, a Gypsy, or an Egyptian read the *Corriere della Sera* or *La Repubblica*! The only thing the immigrants read is *Porta Portese*, for the want ads. As he was leaving, I told him that I admired Montanelli for his courage, his honesty, and his frankness, and because he defied the Red Brigades when they shot him, saying, "You're crazy! Goddam sons of bitches!" I said that in my view Montanelli was wrong when he declared that "the Italian people don't have a historical memory." That may be valid for the rest of Italy but not for Rome, because the people of Rome have a deep-rooted memory that goes back to the ancient Romans. You only have to walk the streets and admire the ruins or glance at our team's banner to find the image of the wolf suckling Romulus and Remus. Finally I remembered my father's advice for winning customers:

"My name is Sandro, what about you?"

"My name is Amede'."

"So you're from Rome?"

"I'm from the south."

When he was about to go I said, "See you tomorrow, Amedeo," and he responded with a warm smile.

Amedeo made an excellent impression from that first encounter, but his answer "I'm from the south," worried me a bit. I'm not a racist, but I can't bear Neapolitans. I hoped from the bottom of my heart that he had nothing to do with Naples, because I still haven't forgotten the beating I got some years ago from the Naples fans after a tie on their home field. I say they didn't deserve a player like Maradona. You know how things ended up for poor Diego? After he won so many trophies they accused him of collusion with the Camorra and then they drove him into drug addiction, until he became more passionate about drugs than about the ball! If Maradona had played for Roma he could have become a man venerated like the Pope. I'm not embarrassed to say "I wouldn't trust a Neapolitan, even if he was San Gennaro!"

Amedeo began coming to the bar every morning for the three "C"s: cappuccino, *cornetto*, *Corriere della Sera*. I tried to learn the details of his origins, his family, his team and political preferences, but Amedeo doesn't talk much, and that made it difficult. The fact is I'm not good at playing cat and mouse, and my patience runs out quickly. So, straight out, I asked him, "Excuse me, Amede', tell me yes or no: are you from Naples?"

"No."

"Are you a fan of Lazio?"

"No."

I drew a sigh of relief and embraced him the way our fans do when Roma scores the winning goal in overtime, and I decided that breakfast was on me that day.

Once I reassured myself that he wasn't Neapolitan or a fan of Lazio, I opened up to him, and we became friends. Our friendship intensified when I bought an apartment in the same building where he lives. I never asked him where he was born or when he came to Rome, but as time passed I discovered that he knows this city better than I do. Surely he must have come here as a small child, like my grandfather, who left Sicily a century ago and settled in the capital. After a while Amedeo became a fan of Roma, and he doesn't miss a game at the Olympic Stadium. It's all thanks to me. I'm an apostle like St. Paul, but with a small difference: I make converts to the Roman faith, whereas he was recruiting for the Catholic Church. When you get right down to it, every fan roots for his home team.

But no! Amedeo wasn't an extremist. I read in some newspaper that the Gladiator who was found murdered in the elevator was a Lazio fan, and the author of the article deduced that they should look for the murderer in neighborhoods with concentrations of Roma fans. But do you really think that's a motive for murder? Rome is innocent. I mean, Amedeo has nothing to do with this horrible crime. Amedeo is good and generous, "good as bread," we say in Rome. For example, he is very generous with the Iranian, he helps him find jobs and pays for his wine. The thing that's notable is Amedeo's passion for penalties—he prefers a penalty kick to a goal! He trembles when a player is about to kick a penalty, I've never understood why.

I find it hard to believe what you're telling me. Amedeo is an immigrant like Parviz the Iranian, Iqbal the Bangladeshi, Maria Cristina the fat maid, Abdu the fish seller, and the Dutch kid who makes me laugh when he repeats like a parrot, "I am not *gentile*." You don't know Amedeo the way I do. He knows the history of Rome and its streets better than I do, in fact better than Riccardo Nardi, who's so proud of his origins, which go back to the ancient Romans. Riccardo, who drives a taxi and has been going up and down the streets of Rome every day for twenty years. Once he and Amedeo had a contest to see who knew the streets better. I was like the MC of a TV quiz show, and I posed a series of questions, for example: Where is Via Sandro Veronese? Where is Via Valsolda? How to you get from Piazza del Popolo to Via Spartaco? Where is Piazza Trilussa? And Piazzale della Radio? And the Foreign Ministry? And the French Embassy? And the Mignon cinema? Via del Babuino? Piazza Mastai? Amedeo answered before Riccardo. When it comes to the history of Rome, Amedeo has no equal, he knows the origins of the street names and their meanings. I've never in my life seen a person like him. Once, after yet another defeat by Amedeo, Riccardo said to him laughing, "Wow, Amede', you really know Rome! Did the wolf suckle you?"

Don't say that Amedeo is an immigrant, it gives me a headache. I don't hate foreigners. Wasn't the greatest player of all time, Paulo Roberto Falcao, a foreigner? What about Piedone, Cerezo, and Voeller, weren't they foreigners? These players were the glory of Roma, and so they deserve respect, appreciation, and esteem. There's a big difference between Rome and Naples, between Rome and Milan, between Rome and Turin. We're friendly with the immigrants, we treat them affectionately. I don't love the people of the north, because they've got the wealth of the whole country. Bastards! They only think of their own interests. Take the example of Antonio Marini, who treats the residents of the building like nursery-school children or a tribe of Zulus. He never stops giving orders. He came from Milan to teach at the University of Rome, as if this were a city of asses, as if we didn't have university professors here, those bastards! They know all about favoritism and influence, they're obsessed with power, with imposing their will on everyone.

That professor from Milan has done his best to keep us from using the elevator; he wanted to have it just for himself, and he advanced the oddest proposals, on the pretext that they would improve the quality of the service: bolt the elevator door shut, keep visitors and guests from using it, ban smoking and spitting, clean your shoes before entering, put in a mirror and a seat for two people, and so on. Once, after yet another meeting where I was really pissed off, I said to him, "You're a pain in the ass, and I've got a mind to beat you up—this elevator belongs to everybody! It's not part of your house, this is our building and we're not a tribe of Zulus! Go back to Milan and do whatever the fuck you like!" He didn't take that: "You barbarians, I'll never be one of you! I will defend civilization in this building as long as I live. The elevator is the dividing line between barbarism and civilization." He should be thrown in jail on charges of defamation, or, at least, expelled from within the walls of Rome, and forbidden to re-enter for the rest of his life. Let's talk about the disgraceful scandals that the Clean Hands investigation has turned up, exposing the corruption in the cities of the north, starting with Milan? And after all this, people still wonder: why has Rome won only two championships while Milan, Inter, and Juventus have won most of the trophies in Italy and abroad? The answer is obvious: corruuuuuuuuuuuuption!

Anyway, I don't agree that soccer should be considered just a simple game, an entertainment. Soccer is a school of life, it teaches you seriousness, patience, application, love of victory, and how to fight to the last second. You remember the end of the Champion's League match between Bayern Munich and Manchester United? Bayern was winning one to nothing right up until the final minute and then Manchester managed to tie and then score the winning goal before the whistle. I've had a lot of arguments with my wife on account of our only son, Pippo, because she claims I'm encouraging him to leave school. I say to her, "You're an idiot! You still believe in school? Don't you see what's happening in the schools—murder, rape, kidnapping?" She says you see all this in the movies, and in some black schools in America. At that point I added, "Remember, love, our models always come from America. Soon you'll be seeing on TV, live, murders carried out in schools by the students themselves—little monsters, as they're called in the newspapers." I have the right to educate my son as I want, I have his future at heart. And then a soccer player earns millions while college graduates just lengthen the lines of the unemployed. No, school is useless, it's really a waste of time.

When I was a boy I went with Uncle Carlo to the stadium to see Roma. He was a fan of Manfredini Pedro Waldemar, called Piedone, Big Foot, because he wore size 14 shoes. Uncle Carlo liked to say, "A match without Piedone is like a Sergio Leone film without Clint Eastwood." Piedone was outstanding! Obviously Manfredini known as Piedone has nothing to do with Manfredini known as the Gladiator. That should be clear, let's not have any confusion.

Then, I don't deny that I quarreled with the Gladiator, like all the residents of the building. He provoked everyone with his outrageous behavior. For example, he thought it was funny to draw pictures and write vulgar words and insults against Roma in the elevator. I warned him, but he stubbornly kept it up. I say again: Amedeo has nothing to do with the murder. I'm utterly certain he's innocent and I'm ready to swear to it.

EIGHTH WAIL

Thursday March 27, 10:39 P.M.

This morning I met the owner of the Bar Dandini. His name is Sandro, and he's around fifty. He told me that Rome is human memory, the city that teaches us every morning that life is eternal spring and death a passing cloud. Rome has defeated death, and that's why it's called the eternal city. Something to remember: when Sandro asked me my name I answered, "Ahmed." But he pronounced it without the letter "h," because "h" isn't used much in Italian, and in the end he called me Amede', which is an Italian name and can be shortened to Amed.

Friday January 27, 11:42 P.M.

I've become a fundamentalist believer in the trio cappuccino, *cornetto*, and *Corriere della Sera*! I really love *cornetti*. Sandro's bar is my first stop on the way to work. My relationship to cappuccino is like a car's to gas: I have to fill up to keep running strong all day. Tonight I read an article in *L'espresso* by a psychologist who advises people to change their name every so often, because it creates an equilibrium among the various personalities that live in conflict within each of us. He said that changing our name helps us to a happier life, because it lightens the burden of memory. So I should be safe from schizophrenia—the name Amedeo won't hurt me. But is there a silent conflict between Amedeo and Ahmed? I'll look for the answer in wailing: Auuuuuu . . .

Saturday February 25, 11:08 P.M.

Sandro likes to imitate television quiz-show hosts. Often I'm one of the contestants. The questions focus on Roman street names and Roman history. I didn't realize that I possessed all this information about Rome. The credit goes to my feet. I love walking, I hate the metro, buses, cars, and elevators, I can't bear the crowds. I love to walk, to enjoy the beauty of Rome in utter calm; hurry is a lover's enemy. I'm patient. I dream of drinking from every fountain in Rome, of discovering the most hidden corners of the city.

Sunday May 7, 11:37 P.M.

Today I went with Sandro to the Olympic Stadium to see a match between Roma and Parma. I'm not happy, in spite of Roma's victory, 2–0, because I didn't see even one penalty kick. How lovely it is to see a player facing the goalie, one man against another, a decisive challenge from which one emerges conqueror or conquered, alive or dead! The penalty is the gladiator's death blow, and the Olympic Stadium is like the Coliseum, where seventy thousand spectators gathered centuries ago.

Sunday June 4, 10:59 P.M.

Sandro told me that Naples fans can't stand the Olympic Stadium because of the banners of the Roma fans, which display a special welcome. For example, last year during the Roma-Naples game there was a banner that said "Welcome, Naples fans, welcome to Italy!" Romans don't much trust Neapolitans, like the concierge Benedetta.

Wednesday July 7, 10:42 P.M.

This morning, while I was sitting drinking my cappuccino, an Italian woman asked Sandro where Via di Ripetta was and he turned to me for help like a man who's been shipwrecked. I told the woman that the metro was the best way to get there, that she should get out at the Flaminia station, near Piazza del Popolo, and that Via di Ripetta was just a few steps away. At that point I remembered something Riccardo the taxidriver said to me: "Amedeo, you were suckled by the wolf!" By now I know Rome as if I had been born here and never left. I have the right to wonder: am I a bastard like the twins Romulus and Remus or an adopted son? The basic question is: how to be suckled by the wolf without being bitten. Now, at least, I ought to perfect the wail, like a real wolf: Auuuuuuuuuuu . . .

Saturday October 22, 11:44 P.M.

This morning Sandro talked to me about the problem of the declining birth rate in Italy. According to him it's the government's fault, because it offers no incentives to young couples. Then he went on at length about the phenomenon of "little monsters"; that is, children who kill parents, brothers, sisters, and other kids their age. At the end he said, "Having children is a ruinous decision. It's like having stocks, when they lose their value you won't find a buyer. No one listens to the Pope and the President of the Republic, when they exhort Italians to have children, and that's because the cost is high, the risks immense, and the benefits few."

THE TRUTH ACCORDING
TO STEFANIA MASSARO

Who is the real Amedeo? I must say, that's a strange question. There isn't a real Amedeo and a fake Amedeo. There is only one Amedeo: that magnificent man who loved me and whom I loved. One day I read a very short definition of love: love is sacrifice. Amedeo sacrificed everything for me. He gave up his country, his language, his culture, his name, and his memory. He did everything possible to make me happy. He learned Italian for me, he loved Italian cooking for me, he called himself Amedeo for me, in other words he became an Italian to be close to me. Believe me, there is no comparison between our story and Erich Segal's *Love Story*!

I've worked in a travel agency in Piazza della Repubblica for ten years. I love everything that has to do with travel. As a child I traveled a lot with my parents and my brother Roberto, but the most absolutely wonderful trip was one we took to the Sahara. I was seduced by the Tuareg, I clung to them like a baby to its mother's breast. When it was time to leave I began to cry, refusing to go back to Rome. I wanted to stay there forever, like Isabelle Eberhardt. My job at the agency doesn't prevent me from working a few hours a week as a volunteer teaching Italian to immigrants.

Of course, I remember very well. I saw him sitting in the first row and looking at me with interest, and he followed the lesson with fierce concentration. I don't know why he reminded me of the Sahara. He was fantastic, he answered every question with amazing quickness.

"When did you come to Italy?"

"Three months ago."

"Did you study Italian in your country?"

"No."

In all my years of teaching I've never met a student like him. Then something very important happened: just a week after we first met I dreamed that I was in a tent, in the arms of a man with his face all bandaged, except for his eyes. I looked up and said to him, "Valentino, my love!" He answered, "I'm not Valentino!" I took off the bandage and saw the face of Amedeo. Then he began to kiss me, slowly, and I felt an intense heat, as if my body were lying on the hot sand at midday. How happy I was! I hoped that dream would last forever. The next day, when I saw Amedeo I thanked him for the kisses of the night before, then I told him the dream in every detail, and he said to me, "It's lovely when a dream comes true entirely, or even only in part." At which I ventured, "Shall we go to the Sahara, retire to a beautiful tent, and make the other parts of the dream come true?" And he answered, "I would like to have the dream in stages, not all at once. For example, it would be enough for me to kiss you now to convince myself that I've set foot in the dream." He took my hand, then he embraced me with a surpassing sweetness. After a few days my bedroom became a beautiful tent. The dream was transformed into reality.

I asked Amedeo insistently to come and live with me in my apartment in Piazza Vittorio, and he hesitated a while before agreeing. I've thought many times of moving, of leaving that building. I can't bear Benedetta, she's a gossip, a big mouth, and above all she's hated me since I was a child and she would blame me for everything that went wrong in the building. She said I rang the doorbells to annoy the tenants, and left the elevator door open. As if I were the only child in all of Piazza Vittorio! I don't like Professor Antonio Marini, because he's like a traffic cop who does nothing but give orders and hand out fines right and left. I don't like my neighbor Elisabetta Fabiani: that stupid woman had no qualms about giving the name of the mythical Valentino to her dog, who won't stop howling, like a wolf on the plains. Once she accused me of being a racist. All you have to do is defend your rights and they stick the label of racist on you! I don't know why she hasn't yet blamed me for the disappearance of her dog.

I know that Amedeo speaks Italian better than many Italians. It's his own doing, his will and his curiosity. I have nothing to do with this miracle, although it's usually attributed to me. Amedeo is self-taught, all you have to know is that he called the Zingarelli dictionary his baby bottle. He was really like a baby attached to its mother's breast. He would read aloud to improve his accent and didn't mind when I corrected his pronunciation. He wasn't bored by consulting the dictionary to understand difficult words. Italian was his daily bread.

Three months after our first meeting we decided to get married. Why wait? We loved each other. Before our marriage Amedeo begged me not to ask him anything about his past. I still remember his words: "My love, my memory is like a broken elevator. Or rather, the past is like a sleeping volcano. Let's try not to wake it, so we can avoid eruptions." I said to him, "Amedeo, my love, I don't want the past. I want your present and our future." Only now am I opening my eyes to this truth: I don't know who Amedeo is. Who was he before he came to Rome? Why did he abandon his native country? Why did he choose Rome? What does his past hide? What secret do the nightmares that haunt him conceal? A mystery that envelops his previous life—maybe that's the secret of my passion for him. One of the most beautiful stages of love is meeting, when one dives into the sea of love without bothering about details or asking dull questions.

I confess that our relationship hasn't gone beyond courtship—there's nothing boring or routine about it. "Passion is a box full of surprises": that's the beginning of a good song. Some lovers are limited by the temptation to want to know everything about one another. This is the cause of the boredom that can kill passion in an instant. The true lover doesn't reveal himself entirely. You know why the Tuareg inspire admiration and amazement? Because they don't uncover their faces. Mystery is the secret of the gods. The fantastic is mysterious by nature. I feel sorry for women who say, "I know my husband perfectly," or "I'm jealous of my boyfriend, I don't take my eyes off him for a second!" I often wonder: what does love have to do with control and police surveillance? I can't bear details, because they keep us from dreaming and fantasizing.

Amedeo doesn't like the past. Often he says to me that the past resembles quicksand: there's no escape. Amedeo is as mysterious as the Sahara, and it's difficult to grasp the secrets of the Sahara. Once I heard an old woman in Mali utter words that I've treasured like rare pearls: "Never trust a guide to the Sahara. He is like Satan, cursed forever, because the Sahara doesn't like arrogance. Those who claim to know it must expect the inevitable punishment, death

from thirst. Modesty is the only language the Sahara under-
stands." A few years ago I met an Icelandic tourist who told
me something extraordinary: that fishermen in the region
where he lives don't know how to swim, because the safety
of a shipwrecked man depends not on knowing how to
swim but on obedience, submission, total resignation to the
sea. There is no difference between the sea and the Sahara.

I'm not ashamed of not knowing Amedeo well in spite of
the years we've spent together. It's an open-ended journey
full of stupendous surprises and fantastic discoveries. I've
worked for a long time with tourists from all over the world,
and in my opinion the problem of tourists lies in their exces-
sive desire to discover everything, and know it, in a few
days. I often advise travelers to be patient, not to be in a
hurry. The best journey doesn't end, because it preserves
within itself the promise of a new beginning for the next
one. It's like the stories of Scheherazade, which never end,
but are always beginning. The beautiful Scheherazade man-
ages to save herself from the revenge of the sultan Shahryar,
who has been betrayed by his wife, through the stories of
the *Thousand and One Nights*. At the rooster's crow she
leaves the story unfinished, to take it up again the following
night. That's how she saved herself and the other women
from death.

Amedeo has suffered from stomach aches for as long as
I've known him. Before going to bed he shuts himself in the
bathroom. He's had lots of tests, but without conclusive
results. All the doctors who've seen him say his stomach is
healthy. He's in the habit of staying shut in the little bathroom for a long time every night, he takes a tape recorder so
he can listen to music, to relax his nerves and settle his
insides, he says. I read in a scientific magazine that the Arab

doctor Avicenna cured his patients with music. Every so often Amedeo has nightmares. I've never asked him about them, because "the nightmare is the window through which the past enters like a thief," as a French writer says.

I've often heard him utter incomprehensible words. Once he woke up frightened, repeating, "Bagia! Bagia!" He was sweating as if he had escaped from Hell. The next day I couldn't contain my curiosity and I asked him the meaning of the word Bagia. He didn't answer but looked at me reproachfully, perhaps to remind me of the agreement we made before our marriage: the past is like a volcano, be careful not to rouse it! The word Bagia has gotten stuck in my memory, though, and I've tried to find out what it means. I've asked some Arab clients who come to the agency, but I haven't unraveled the mystery.

No. I say that there is no connection between the death of Lorenzo and the disappearance of Amedeo. I'm sure that Amedeo is innocent. There is not a single motive that might have led him to commit such a terrible act. The Gladiator was not liked by the building's residents, everyone knows that. He was mean to everyone without ever apologizing. It's not right to accuse Amedeo like this. Ask the people of Piazza Vittorio about Amedeo and you'll see how much he was loved by everyone. He didn't hesitate to help those who needed it, without expecting any reward.

For example, Amedeo managed to persuade the Bangladeshis to send their wives to school. He successfully completed a difficult mission. For these women the school provides an occasion to meet each other, to talk, to get out of their houses. It's a real motivation for leaving their prison. Many of them—far from home, in a strange culture—suffer tremendously from solitude, yet they stay in Italy because a ticket home is expensive, and they can't afford it. Many Bangladeshis return to their country every five years or even less frequently. Talking is useful for letting out their sadness, anguish, homesickness, for lamenting the absence of loved ones. The men are extremely closed off, they live as if they were in Dhaka, they eat rice and wear Bangladeshi clothes and watch videos. I often wonder: do they really live in Rome?

I don't know where Amedeo is now, I'm afraid something has happened to him. I still look for him everywhere—I hope he's all right. There are so many questions surrounding his disappearance, because of this terrible accusation of murder. But I am an optimist, and I'm sure he's innocent. I will defend him to the very end, without giving up!

NINTH WAIL

Sunday June 4, 10:33 P.M.
I'm like a newborn, I need milk every day. Italian is my daily milk. Stefania is life; that is, the present and the future. I love Stefania because she is closely attached to life, I adore her memory free of nightmares. I want to be infected by life, love, future, and a happy wail. Auuuuuuuu . . .

Monday November 17, 11:57 P.M.
So many people consider their work a daily punishment. Whereas I love my work as a translator. Translation is a journey over a sea from one shore to the other. Sometimes I think of myself as a smuggler: I cross the frontiers of language with my booty of words, ideas, images, and metaphors.

Wednesday September 29, 11:09 P.M.
Poor Stefania, she's worried about me, she thinks I'm suffering from stomach pains. The problem is that the stomach of my memory hasn't yet digested everything I swallowed before coming to Rome. Memory is just like a stomach. Every so often it makes me vomit. I vomit memories of blood non-stop. I have an ulcer in my memory. Is there a cure? Yes: wailing! Auuuuuuuuu . . .

Sunday March 9, 11:17 P.M.

Today I finished reading Amin Maalouf's novel *Leo Africanus*. I reread this passage over and over until I knew it by heart:" I, Hassan, son of Muhammad the weigh-master, I, Jean-Leon de' Medici, circumcised at the hand of a barber and baptized at the hand of a Pope, I am now called the African, but I am not from Africa, nor from Europe, nor from Arabia . . . I'm the son of the road. My country is the caravan. My life the most unexpected of voyages." It's marvelous to be able to free ourselves from the chains of identity which lead us to ruin. Who am I? Who are you? Who are they? These are pointless and stupid questions.

Thursday November 18, 10:51 P.M.

Stefania is very pleased at having started teaching Italian to the Bangladeshi women. Yesterday she said to me, "Soon we'll establish the first Bangladeshi feminist organization in Italy!" I told her that that wasn't the agreement. She laughed, adding, "Don't you remember that Louis Aragon quote? 'Woman is the future of man.'" I said, "Soon I'll be like *le fou d'Elsa:* Stefania's madman." I love Stefania because she is my future.

Thursday February 2, 11:13 P.M.

Today I started reading the aphorisms of Emil Cioran. I was struck by this one: "We inhabit not a country but a language." Is the Italian language my new dwelling place? Auu-uuuu . . .

Saturday October 24, 10:45 P.M.

Stefania is never tired of seeing *The Sheikh,* with Rudolf Valentino. I've seen her weep sometimes, with emotion.

Maybe it reminds her of her father, who died in a drilling accident in Libya several years ago. Her father was an expert at finding oil. Stefania believes that the word "expert" was his curse. She always says to me that the Sahara has no pity for those who do not show respect for it.

Thursday June 24, 10:57 P.M.

The damn nightmare is pursuing me. Stefania told me this morning that I cried out in my sleep and that I kept repeating the name Bagia. I didn't want to tell her the details. It's pointless for her to join the game of nightmares. My memory is wounded and bloody: I have to heal the wounds of the past in solitude. A shame, Bagia shows up only in nightmares, wrapped in a bloodstained sheet. Oh, this open wound that will never heal! I have no consolation but wailing. Auuuuuu . . .

Sunday March 30, 11:48 P.M.

This morning I reread the novel *The Invention of the Desert* by the Algerian writer Tahar Djaout. I paused for a long time on this sentence: "Happy people have neither age nor memory, they have no need of the past." I'm going to wail all night long in search of consolation: Auuuuu . . .

The Truth According
to Abdallah Ben Kadour

W hy did he call himself Amedeo? That's the question that leaves me so perplexed. His real name
is Ahmed, which is a precious name, because it's
one of the names of the prophet Mohammed—it's mentioned both in the Koran and in the Gospels. Frankly I
don't much appreciate people who change their name or
deny their origins: for example, my name is Abdallah, and I
know perfectly well that it's a difficult name for Italians to
pronounce, but in spite of that I've sworn not to change it
as long as I live. I don't want to disobey my father, who gave
me this name, or God, who forbids us to disobey our parents. Changing your name is a capital crime, like murder,
adultery, bearing false witness, like stealing from orphans.
Many Italians I know have tried to persuade me to change
my name, proposing a series of Italian names like Alessandro, Francesco, Massimiliano, Guido, Mario, Luca, Pietro,
and others, but I have resolutely refused. The problem
doesn't end there. Some have used a trick that's very common in Rome, which consists of eliminating the first or second part of a name. So I've been called Abd, which means
"slave," or even Allah! I've asked forgiveness from God
because He forgives all sins except polytheism. I've tried to
keep my composure as I explain to them that all men,
including the prophets and the messengers of God, are His

servants, and so my name has nothing to do with the kind of slavery that was everywhere in the time of Kunta Kinte. So I found myself caught between two fires: either fall into the trap of polytheism every time someone called me Allah or endure the insults of those who called me Abd. Finally I found a way out of this impasse, thanks to my Egyptian friend Metwali, who advised me to make a small change in my name. He told me that the Egyptians have a custom of calling Abdu people whose name begins with Abd: Abdrahman, Abdalkarim, Abdkader, Abdrahim, Abdjabar, Abdhakim, Abdsabour, Abdaraouf. I agreed, because this solution avoided the problems I've mentioned. Unfortunately there are some people who have first and last names steeped in polytheism. Take Iqbal, the Bangladeshi. I've told him many times that his last name, Amir Allah, is polytheistic. If he knew Arabic, he would understand that there is no difference between Amir Allah and Amir "superior to Allah." God save us from Satan!

I will not change my skin, or my religion, or my country, or my name, for any reason. I'm proud of myself, I'm not like those immigrants who change their name to please the Italians. Take the Tunisian who works in the restaurant Luna at the station. His real name is Mohsen, but he's had himself called, or they called him, Massimiliano. God says in the Koran: "Jews and Christians will not accept you until you follow their religion." God the Great is right. I can't bear it when people deny their origins. You know the story of the donkey who when he's asked, Who is your father?, answers, "The horse is my uncle"? You know about the crow that wanted to imitate the dove's way of walking and, after various futile attempts, decides to go back to his natural way and at that point discovers that he no longer remembers it?

Amedeo is from my neighborhood. I know him very well, just as I know his whole family. His younger brother was one of my dearest friends, my schoolmate and playmate. Ahmed was a person who was loved and respected in the neighborhood. I don't recall that he ever fought, although there were frequent brawls among gangs, which are a widespread phenomenon in the neighborhoods of Algiers. Ahmed's troubles began when his fiancée, Bagia, died; she was the neighbors' daughter. Ahmed had loved her since he was a child, and wanted to marry her, but unfortunately things turned out differently. Bagia, which in Arabic means "joy," is a female name, and a name, too, for Algiers.

One day Bagia went to see her sister in Boufarik, not far from Algiers, and on the way back the bus was stopped by terrorists who had set up a fake checkpoint, passing themselves off as police. They cut the throats of all the passengers except the girls. Bagia tried to flee, to avoid being raped, so they shot her in a burst of machine-gun fire. Ahmed couldn't accept that tragedy. He shut himself in the house for days, then he disappeared. In the neighborhood various hypotheses made the rounds: some said that he had enlisted in the army, seeking revenge against the fundamentalists, some maintained that he had joined the armed fighters in the mountains as a sign of rejection and condemnation of the state, some said that he had gone off to join a Sufi sect in the Sahara and live like the Tuareg, and finally someone said that Ahmed had gone mad and was wandering, naked, through the streets. One neighbor even assured his family that he had recognized Ahmed at the station in Annaba, in the eastern part of the country, waiting for a train to Tunisia. I never understood why his family didn't resort to a well-known television show, *Everything Is Possible*, which looks for missing people. One day I asked his mother, Aunt Fatma Zohra, for news of Ahmed, and she said sharply, "He's outside." The word "outside" has a thousand meanings: outside of reason, outside of Algiers, outside the law, outside the charity of his parents, outside the grace of God. I preferred not to insist and left the cover on the well, as our old proverb goes.

Then one day I saw him in the market in Piazza Vittorio, where I sell fish: I called to him, "Ahmed! Ahmed!," but he didn't respond. It seemed to me that he was pretending not to recognize me. Finally he greeted me, but coldly. He was with an Italian woman, only later did I find out that she was his wife. We met often at the Bar Dandini. He wasn't enthusiastic about hearing the latest news from Algeria, so I decided to avoid talking to him on subjects that had to do with our country—I didn't want to upset him. I didn't even dare to advise him to give up the name Amedeo and return to his original name, Ahmed, which is the name of the Prophet, peace be upon him. It's said that returning to one's origins is a virtue!

Ahmed or Amedeo—as you call him—worked at the Supreme Court in Algiers as a translator from French into Arabic. He had bought an apartment in Bab Azouar for him and Bagia to live in after their marriage, but destiny held another life in store for him. As you see, the story of Ahmed Salmi is simple, it's not that complicated. The truth is different, it's not what you thought up to now. There are no particular secrets, no twisted events in his life before he settled in Rome.

I've sold fish for years, and I find no difference between the lives of fish and the lives of immigrants. I know a proverb that the Italians often repeat: "Guests are like fish, after three days they stink." The immigrant is a guest, no more or less, and, like fish, you eat him when he's fresh and throw him in the garbage when he loses his color. There are two types of immigrants: the fresh ones, who are exploited inhumanly in the factories of the north or the agricultural lands of the south, and the frozen, who fill the freezers and are used only in an emergency. You know what Gianfranco, the owner of the shop where I work, calls the girls from Eastern Europe who sell their bodies for a little money: fresh fish!

Gianfranco is over sixty, he is married and has four children older than me. His favorite hobby is to drive out on the Appia Antica at night in search of girls from Nigeria or Eastern Europe, girls who are at most twenty and often much younger. So he spends a peaceful hour with the fresh fish—so he calls the girl of the moment—before returning to the arms of his wife, whom he makes fun of with his friends, calling her a frozen fish, who always needs a little time to thaw and warm up before being consumed. Gianfranco, or the Pig—as his friends call him—likes to sit in front of the shop all day with them and, before the astonished gaze of his customers, recount in detail his adventures of the night before. Often enthusiastic laughter greets him, followed by obscene comments like "Gianfranco, you're a pig! Gianfranco, you're a fat pig!" And the cad isn't bothered by that odious nickname, because the pig is the symbol of virility in Italy. In fact, he's proud of it!

I haven't changed the subject, I'm still talking about Ahmed. If I heard someone call me Pig I would cut out his tongue, because the pig or *halouf*—as we call it—is hateful and has nothing to do with virility and masculinity. In fact, it's the worst insult. The pig is a dirty animal, it lives in the garbage. I don't understand why there hasn't been an outbreak of mad-pig disease. Why has that dangerous disease affected only cows? It's a perplexing question.

In Rome there is the Termini station. "Termini" means terminal, the journey is over. There's something strange about this city. It's very difficult to leave. Maybe the water in the fountains is mixed with a special substance that has magical origins.

Have you seen the difference between us and them? Ahmed hasn't grasped the substantial differences between our religion and Gianfranco's. I can still remember the fear that struck me when I heard people call him Amedeo. I was afraid he had renounced Islam. I didn't hesitate an instant, I asked him with distress and concern, "Ahmed, have you converted to Christianity?" And he answered serenely, "No." I sighed deeply and said aloud, "Praise be to God! Praise be to God!" My fears were legitimate, because usually someone who changes his name has embraced a new religion, like the famous English singer Cat Stevens who had people call him Yousef Islam right after his conversion.

Don't you see what the newspapers are saying about Ahmed? As soon as they discovered that he was an immigrant and not an Italian they didn't hesitate to accuse him of murder. Certainly, Ahmed made a mistake by swimming outside his natural harbor. His disappearance reminds me so much of his disappearance years ago, which caused such dismay in our neighborhood. The question is the same today: what happened to Ahmed, or Amedeo—as you call him?

Saturday March 25, 10:56 P.M.

What's the difference between a dove and a raven? Am I a raven that wants to imitate a dove? What is wailing? There are two types of wailing, one for grief and one for happiness. Many of the alienated immigrants hugging their bottles of wine and beer in the gardens in Piazza Vittorio never stop wailing sadly, because the wolf's bite is painful. Every so often the wailing is like weeping. I, on the other hand, wail with joy, immense joy. I suckle on the wolf with the two orphans Romulus and Remus. I adore the wolf, I can't do without her milk.

Monday January 21, 11:15 P.M.

When he called out to me—"Ahmed!"—I didn't recognize him right away. I felt a hand on my shoulder and I tried to remember. "I'm Abdallah, from your neighborhood. Your brother Farid's friend." I barely remembered the neighborhood, my brother Farid, Algeria. Greeting me he said, "I'll see you next Friday at the big mosque, then we'll go together to a Moroccan restaurant nearby to eat couscous." At that point I remembered how once, overwhelmed by homesickness for couscous, I went to an Arabic restaurant, and after a few bites I threw up. Only afterward did it occur to me that couscous is like mother's milk, and has a special odor that has to be inhaled accompanied by hugs and kisses.

Wednesday September 5, 11:27 P.M.

It's sad spending Ramadan far away from Bagia! What's the point of giving up eating and drinking, only to eat alone? Where is the voice of the muezzin? Where is the *buraq*? Where is the couscous that Mama prepared with her own hands? Where is the *qalb alluz*? Where is the *zlabia*? Where is the *harira*? Where is the *maqrout*? How can I forget the nights of Ramadan in the neighborhood, and coming home late? Mama's voice full of tenderness, the love that charmed my ears: "My son, it's time for the *suhur*." The month of Ramadan, the Little Feast, the Big Feast, and the other feasts fill my heart with anxiety. People say: "Why don't you go to the big mosque in Rome for the prayers for the Big Feast?" No, thank you. I don't want to see hundreds of needy people like me, needy for the odor of their loved ones.

Friday October 25, 11:22 P.M.

Tomorrow the end of Ramadan is celebrated. Of course my mother will weep because of my absence. On days like this the distance increases and the warmth of the feelings of our loved ones grows cold. I'll call her tomorrow with good wishes, as I always do on these occasions. I know she'll reproach me a little at first, as she always does, then she'll pray for me. How I long to hear her say these words: "Ahmed, my son, may your feast be blessed and may you be well every year."

Tuesday March 20, 11:15 P.M.

I have the flu, I can't get up. Illness stirs up the devil of homesickness, or the beast—as we call it—that is the fear of dying: dying far from the eyes of our dear ones, dying alone, dying far from our mother. "How can I tell my mother I'm afraid?" De André wonders in a song of his. Isn't eternal rest a return to the mother's womb? What anguish is a tomb that holds your remains in exile! Auuuuuuu . . .

Saturday April 26, 2:14 A.M.

The guest of the shadows woke me a little while ago, the same nightmare that visits every so often. I can't get back to sleep. What is the nightmare? The nightmare is a fierce dog. My grandfather was a peasant, who never left his village in the mountains of Djurdjura, and he would say to me, "When a dog sniffs you, don't run away, stand still and look him in the eye. You'll see, he'll back off. Instead, if you run away he'll run after you and bite you." I don't run away from my nightmares. I look them in the face, remembering all the details. I challenge them fearlessly, because the toilet is the nightmare's tomb. Here's the nightmare in its full version:

I see . . . I see myself emerging from the hole of life covered with blood. The hearts of my relatives are pounding. Courage, mama! My mother fights the birth pains, struggles to lift her head. Before drying my tears and planting the first kisses on my red cheeks, my mother glances with anguish and anxiety below my navel. Now she heaves a long sigh. God and the saints have heard her prayer.

"*Dhakar! Dhakar! Dhakar!*"[1]

"Yuuuuyuuuuuyuuuuuuuuuuuu…"

So I greet life with tears, and it, life, welcomes me with *zagharid*.[2] It doesn't matter if the newborn *dhakar* is hand-

---

[1] In Arabic *dhakar* means both male and penis.
[2] A sharp, typically female ululation that emphasizes particular moments of joy.

some or not. It doesn't matter if the newborn is healthy or sick. It doesn't matter if the unborn child . . . it doesn't matter . . . it doesn't matter. What matters is that it is a *dhakar*. What matters is that I am a *dhakar*. Rather, what counts in the end is not me. What really counts is my *dhakar*.

I see . . . I see my *dhakar* or the *dhakar* of my family grow until the moment of circumcision. I will see my blood flow and I'll curse the *zagharid* that suffocate my sobs. I'll remember the *zagharid* of birth again, and again see my blood falling, drop by drop, on the ground. Why did they cut the throat of the *dhakar*? They call it the festival of purification! For them singing, dancing, and joy; for me pain, tears, and suffering: what hurts me is the fact that I wasn't consulted. But to whom does the *dhakar* belong, me or them? I'll watch the *dhakar* grow, and its secret activities. And quickly the small red head will enter public life with marriage. So my *dhakar* gets married and I'm in trouble. On the wedding night my hatred for those who tricked me will increase.

I see . . . I see myself alone before the wall of virginity. The Chinese wall! The mountains of the Himalayas! How I grieve for the lost years! They told me that adultery is punished with a hundred lashes. They fought me with all their weapons: God, the prophets, the saints, religion, custom, good behavior, people's opinion, AIDS. So we went into the ring like two fighters at their first match. She is afraid and I am, too. The advice, the recommendations will remain outside our bedroom. But she is more afraid than I am. I screw up my courage with a glass or two and some cigarettes. What do I say to her? I won't say anything. My words will encourage her and weaken me. Victim or executioner! There is no other choice. She won't look up. She is more afraid than I am. Will I kiss her? Caress her? What is this hesitation? They're all waiting outside the door. The mouths of the women are filled with *zagharid*. Goddam *zagharid*! The *dhakar* has to penetrate the wall. This is indisputable. It could betray me at the last minute, and I would pay a price that's too high. I don't trust it. I might fall under the spell of evil women who rob men of their virility. I would be struck by the curse of the marbout. But it's not Mr. Dhakar who can save me from this folkloric night. Let's go, onward! The *zagharid* won't be heard if the sacred liquid doesn't flow. The *dhakar* is the knife that cuts virginity. Onward! Blood! Blood! Blood! Blood! Blood! Blood!

"Yuuuuyuuuuuyuuuuuuuuuuuu…"

I see . . . I see myself coming out of the room covered with blood. My family, my wife's family, and the guests assault me like wasps hovering pitilessly over carrion. After a while I feel teeth in my flesh, I see my blood on the ground, I struggle to open my eyes, and see wolves surrounding me on all sides. Auuuuuu . . .

In the meantime an old man with a long white beard passes me without stopping.

"Help me, grandfather."

"I'm not your grandfather."

"Then who are you?"

"I'm Luqmanè."[1]

"Help me, Luqmanè, O wise man."

"Listen to my advice, learn it by heart. My son, if, as you walk, armed men stop you and force you to be the judge, asking you, 'Who is right and who is wrong, Cain or Abel?' woe to you if you answer, 'Cain is right and Abel is wrong.' The armed men might be Abel's men and it will be the end

---

[1] Character cited in the Koran for his wisdom.

of you. Oh my son, woe to you twice if you say that Cain is wrong and Abel is right, because the armed men might be Cain's men, and it will be the end of you. Oh, my son, woe to you three times if you say that neither Cain nor Abel is wrong: it will be the end of you, because our time is very short, and there is no room for neutrality. My son, cut out your tongue and swallow it. Oh, my son, run away! Run away! Run away! Woe to strife, because it's more dangerous than the teeth of wolves. Auuuuu..."

On the crest of this nocturnal wail I woke trembling, I went quickly into the little bathroom and began recording the nightmare's words.

THE TRUTH ACCORDING
TO MAURO BETTARINI

I've learned from my job as a police inspector that the truth is like a coin: it has two faces. The first always completes the second.

The Truth: The First Face

For me the investigation is over. The murderer is Ahmed Salmi, whom everyone calls Amedeo. His sudden disappearance proves his involvement in the killing of young Lorenzo Manfredini, known as the Gladiator. Usually the perpetrator flees. Reality is very different from the movies. It's only Lieutenant Columbo who doesn't have to struggle to find the criminals and arrest them, for the simple reason that in the end they surrender without resistance. Unfortunately, I'm not Columbo, and I have to track down the criminals and then put them in jail.

I was assigned to investigate this murder because I'm well acquainted with the area. I've spent many years at the police station on the Esquiline, and I've had the opportunity to get to know the problems of the residents of Piazza Vittorio. I met Ahmed Salmi or Amedeo when he offered to help resolve the problem with the pigeons in Piazza Santa Maria Maggiore caused by his Iranian friend. I have no doubt, this Iranian is crazy. Once he said to me, "Why do you arrest me for no reason, while when it comes to those delinquents who bother people by eating pizza on the metro you leave them alone?" Shouldn't a man who says something like that be locked up in a mental institution? The accused also asked me a year ago to help an Asian immigrant, I don't remember where he was from, to correct some mistake on his residency permit.

I thought that Amedeo was an Italian volunteer who helped the immigrants with some of their applications regarding health care and jobs. I don't understand why certain Italians make such an effort to help the immigrants. Many others are demanding that criminal immigrants be expelled, since half the prisoners in Italian jails are foreigners. We're between the fire on the right and the fire on the left: the press on the right criticizes us because we are not inflexible toward the immigrants, while the left accuses us of brutality. It's not easy to expel immigrants who commit crimes, because we don't know their real countries or their real names, and, besides, they're used to changing their names and falsifying their identities.

I say we should forbid the showing of police films and TV shows, because they've become a school for training criminals. There are endless formulas for how to go about killing a husband or lover or boss and disposing of the body, and for how to deceive the investigators and avoid falling into the traps of police interrogators. I admit that our job has become arduous and demanding, because the secrets of the work are available to anyone. We've reached the point of bankruptcy. TV be damned! A few days ago a young Dutch fellow came looking for me at headquarters. I agreed to see him, thinking he had some important information on the elevator murder, and I was astonished when he said to me, "Inspector, I am happy to invite you to participate in my new film." I got up like a shot, making an enormous effort to control myself, and began shouting, "Get out! Get out! Get out!" If I had got hold of him at that moment, I would have killed him.

There's a connection between the murder, the sudden disappearance of Amedeo, and the finding of the boy's body in the elevator. We began the investigation first by looking into the disappearance, or rather the flight, of Amedeo, the accused. The question we posed is the following: if Amedeo is innocent, as his neighbors maintain, then why doesn't he show up and defend his innocence? The evidence we gathered from sources, and witnesses increased our suspicions and led us to focus on his guilt. A short time afterward we discovered that he is an immigrant and that his real name is Ahmed Salmi. As I told you, criminals and other lowlives frequently falsify personal details. So we found ourselves, as investigators, facing a double challenge: to gather evidence confirming that Amedeo is an immigrant and evidence that attests to his involvement in the murder.

We thought about his name for a long time; we didn't find the name Amedeo on his official documents: passport, marriage license, residency permit, and so forth. The law doesn't forbid citizens to change their names, on condition that they leave official documents untouched. Ahmed Salmi known as Amedeo didn't falsify any documents. Why did he disappear? Is it simply a coincidence or is he fleeing the law? There are eyewitnesses who saw him quarrel with the victim the day before the murder. No one knows why. They heard him yell at the victim, "I'll kill you if you do it again!" For me the investigation is over. Amedeo is the murderer, and this makes him a wanted man. I hope for his sake that he surrenders as soon as possible.

The Truth: The Second Face

No, the investigation is not over, and Ahmed Salmi nick-named Amedeo is not the murderer of Lorenzo Manfredini, the Gladiator. After the publication of an interview accompanied by my photograph and Amedeo's in a daily paper, I was contacted by Dr. Simonetti at San Camillo hospital, and she asked me to come immediately. I got there quickly, and she took me to the intensive care unit, where I saw Amedeo lying on a bed. The doctor reported to me that on the morning of March 21st, the day Lorenzo Manfredini was murdered, the patient was in an accident while he was crossing a street near the Coliseum, and was rushed to the hospital. Ahmed Salmi has been unconscious since then, having suffered severe brain trauma, as a result of which he may lose his memory. I asked her what time the accident happened, and it turns out that the ambulance got there around eight-thirty. So the accident must have happened about ten minutes earlier. Amedeo is not the murderer, then, because the coroner said that the crime occurred after 1 P.M. Furthermore, eyewitnesses stated that they had seen Manfredini that morning between nine and noon. So there is not the least doubt: Ahmed Salmi known as Amedeo is innocent.

After that, we reviewed the investigation up to that point, leaving aside the question "Who is Amedeo?" to concentrate instead on the Gladiator and the life he led. Within a short time we picked up valuable information about Lorenzo Manfredini. We discovered, for example, that he was hated by all the residents of the building. He came home drunk, he peed in the elevator, he often quarreled with Sandro Dandini and with Antonio Marini. Further, he more than once raped the domestic worker Maria Cristina. The woman didn't dare to report him for fear of being expelled, because she doesn't have a residency permit, and she asked Amedeo to help her; he didn't hesitate to warn Manfredini and even threaten him. This was the reason for the quarrel between Amedeo and Manfredini the night before the murder. Who killed Lorenzo Manfredini? The murderer left no trace at the scene of the crime, and this led us to consider him a professional. Then, there is no doubt that the nickname Gladiator helped us greatly in coming up with the guilty party's name.

We made inquiries about the origin of this nickname. It seems that Lorenzo took bets, organizing clandestine dog fights that always ended with the death of one of the contestants. In the time of the Romans, the gladiator was a prisoner or slave who fought against a wild beast, a lion or tiger, in front of thousands of spectators in the Coliseum. Lorenzo and his companions had invented a new game of death. You remember the disappearance of the dog Valentino a few weeks before the crime? Lorenzo was responsible for this operation. After exhaustive inquiries, Elisabetta Fabiani succeeded in finding out the perpetrator of the theft of her Valentino, and so, once she had ascertained the horrible torture inflicted on her dog before his death, she decided to take a cruel revenge.

She came up with an extremely effective plan, making use of information gleaned from the police shows that she watched on TV every day. She chose the elevator, because it's at the center of the conflicts among the building's residents. Then, to avoid suspicion, she used a knife, because it's considered a typically male weapon. And then she began to wander barefoot around Piazza Vittorio to indicate that she was going mad out of desperation because of the kidnapping of her beloved dog. She managed to carry out her plan with great mastery, apparently leaving no trace. The only mistake she made was not to get rid of the murder weapon, which she kept as a trophy. After a lengthy search, we found the knife, on which traces of the victim's blood remained. The woman wanted to keep something to remind her that Valentino's murderer had got the punishment he deserved. Or maybe she was so sure she had carried out the perfect crime that no one would ever suspect her. Now the investigation is over. Elisabetta Fabiani killed Lorenzo Manfredini known as the Gladiator.

FINAL WAIL
OR *BEFORE THE ROOSTER CROWS*

Monday November 25, 10:36 P.M.

The truth is bitter, like medicine. One must take it in small doses, not all in one gulp, because it can cause death. Truth doesn't wound, as the French say—"*la vérité blesse.*" The truth kills. Whereas wailing is the eternal song of Orpheus. Auuuuuuuuuuuuu . . .

Saturday December 7, 10:55 P.M.

This morning I read a line by René Char: "Are we doomed to be alone at the origins of truth?" I said to myself that the word "truth" must always be accompanied by a question mark or an exclamation point or a parenthesis, or quotation marks, never a period. Auuuuu . . .

Wednesday June 25, 10:19 P.M.

I'm not in the mouth of the wolf, "*la gueule du loup,*" as the Algerian writer Kateb Yacine says. Here I am, in the wolf's arms, so that I may suckle until I'm sated. Auuuuu . . .

Sunday March 16, 11:38 P.M.

Every so often doubt seizes me when I think that I pass for good in the eyes of all. But what do they know about it? Amedeo might be simply a mask! I am a wild animal who can't abandon its primal nature. The truth is that my memory is a wild animal, just like a wolf: Auuuuuu . . .

Thursday April 23, 11:27 P.M.

Am I also Scheherazade? *Scheherazade c'est moi?* She tells stories and I wail. We're both fleeing death, and the night takes us in. Is telling stories useful? We have to tell stories to survive. Damn memory! Memory is the rock of Sisyphus. Who am I? Ahmed or Amedeo? Ah, Bagia! Is there happiness away from your smile? Is there tranquility outside your arms? Could this be the moment of repose? How long will my exile last? How long will my wailing go on? Auuuuuuuuu . . .

Saturday March 23, 11:55 P.M.

Teach me, adored lady, the art of escaping death. Teach me, Scheherazade, how to avoid the rage and hatred of the sultan Shahryar. Teach me how to keep the sword of Shahryar from my neck. Teach me, Scheherazade, how to defeat the Shahryar that is inside me. My memory is Shahryar. Auuu . . . My memory is Shahryar. Auuu . . . My memory is Shahryar. Auuuuuuuuuuuuuuuuu . . .

ABOUT THE AUTHOR

Amara Lakhous was born in Algiers in 1970. He has a degree in philosophy from the University of Algiers and another in cultural anthropology from the University la Sapienza, Rome. He recently completed a PhD thesis entitled "Living Islam as a Minority." His first novel, *Le cimici e il pirata* (*Bedbugs and the Pirate*), was published in 1999. *Clash of Civilizations Over an Elevator in Piazza Vittorio*, winner of Italy's prestigious Flaiano prize for fiction and currently being made into a film, is his second novel. He lives in Italy.

Carmine Abate
Between Two Seas
"Abate populates this magical novel with a cast of captivating, emotionally complex characters."—*Publishers Weekly*
224 pp • $14.95 • ISBN: 978-1-933372-40-2

Stefano Benni
Margherita Dolce Vita
"A modern fable...hilarious social commentary."—*People*
240 pp • $14.95 • ISBN: 978-1-933372-20-4

Timeskipper
"Thanks to Benni we have a renewed appreciation
of the imagination's ability to free us from our increasingly mundane surroundings."—*The New York Times*
400 pp • $16.95 • ISBN: 978-1-933372-44-0

Massimo Carlotto
The Goodbye Kiss
"A masterpiece of Italian noir."—*Globe and Mail*
160 pp • $14.95 • ISBN: 978-1-933372-05-1

Death's Dark Abyss
"A remarkable study of corruption and redemption
in a world where revenge is best served ice-cold."
—*Kirkus* (starred review)
160 pp • $14.95 • ISBN: 978-1-933372-18-1

The Fugitive
"The reigning king of Mediterranean noir."
—*The Boston Phoenix*
176 pp • $14.95 • ISBN: 978-1-933372-25-9

Steve Erickson
Zeroville
"A funny, disturbing, daring and demanding novel—Erickson's best."
—*The New York Times*
352 pp • $14.95 • ISBN: 978-1-933372-39-6

Elena Ferrante
The Days of Abandonment
"The raging, torrential voice of [this] author
is something rare."—*The New York Times*
192 pp • $14.95 • ISBN: 978-1-933372-00-6

Troubling Love
"Ferrante's polished language belies the rawness of her imagery, which
conveys perversity, violence, and bodily functions in ripe detail."
—*The New Yorker*
144 pp • $14.95 • ISBN: 978-1-933372-16-7

The Lost Daughter
"A resounding success…Delicate yet daring, precise
yet evanescent: it hurts like a cut, and cures like balm."
—*La Repubblica*
144 pp • $14.95 • ISBN: 978-1-933372-42-6

Jane Gardam
Old Filth
"Gardam's novel is an anthology of such bittersweet scenes,
rendered by a novelist at the very top of her form."
—*The New York Times*
304 pp • $14.95 • ISBN: 978-1-933372-13-6

The Queen of the Tambourine
"This is a truly superb and moving novel."
—*The Boston Globe*
272 pp • $14.95 • ISBN: 978-1-933372-36-5

The People on Privilege Hill
"Artful, perfectly judged shifts of mood fill *The People on Privilege Hill*
with an abiding sense of joy."—*The Guardian*
208 pp • $15.95 • ISBN: 978-1-933372-56-3

Alicia Giménez-Bartlett
Dog Day
"Delicado and Garzón prove to be one of the more engaging sleuth teams to debut in a long time."—*The Washington Post*
320 pp • $14.95 • ISBN: 978-1-933372-14-3

Prime Time Suspect
"A gripping police procedural."—*The Washington Post*
320 pp • $14.95 • ISBN: 978-1-933372-31-0

Death Rites
304 pp • $16.95 • ISBN: 978-1-933372-54-9

Katharina Hacker
The Have-Nots
"Hacker's prose, aided by Atkins's pristine translation, soars [as] she admirably explores modern urban life from the unsettled haves to the desperate have-nots."—*Publishers Weekly*
352 pp • $14.95 • ISBN: 978-1-933372-41-9

Patrick Hamilton
Hangover Square
"Hamilton is a sort of urban Thomas Hardy: always a pleasure to read, and as social historian he is unparalleled."
—Nick Hornby
336 pp • $14.95 • ISBN: 978-1-933372-06-8

James Hamilton-Paterson
Cooking with Fernet Branca
"Irresistable!"—*The Washington Post*
288 pp • $14.95 • ISBN: 978-1-933372-01-3

Amazing Disgrace
"It's loads of fun, light and dazzling as a peacock feather."
—*New York Magazine*
352 pp • $14.95 • ISBN: 978-1-933372-19-8

Alfred Hayes
The Girl on the Via Flaminia
"Immensely readable."—*The New York Times*
160 pp • $14.95 • ISBN: 978-1-933372-24-2

Jean-Claude Izzo
Total Chaos
"Izzo's Marseilles is ravishing. Every street, cafe
and house has its own character."—*Globe and Mail*
256 pp • $14.95 • ISBN: 978-1-933372-04-4

Chourmo
"A bitter, sad and tender salute to a place equally
impossible to love or to leave."—*Kirkus* (starred review)
256 pp • $14.95 • ISBN: 978-1-933372-17-4

Solea
"[Izzo is] a talented writer who draws from the deep,
dark well of noir."—*The Washington Post*
208 pp • $14.95 • ISBN: 978-1-933372-30-3

The Lost Sailors
"Izzo digs deep into what makes men weep."
—*Time Out New York*
272 pp • $14.95 • ISBN: 978-1-933372-35-8

A Sun for the Dying
"Beautiful, like a black sun, tragic and desperate."—*Le Point*
224 pp • $15.00 • ISBN: 978-1-933372-59-4

Gail Jones
Sorry
"In deft and vivid prose...Jones's gift for conjuring place
and mood rarely falters."—*Times Literary Supplement*
240 pp • $15.95 • ISBN: 978-1-933372-55-6

Matthew F. Jones
Boot Tracks
"I haven't read something that made me empathize with
a bad guy this intensely since I read *In Cold Blood*."
—*The Philadelphia Inquirer*
208 pp • $14.95 • ISBN: 978-1-933372-11-2

Ioanna Karystiani
The Jasmine Isle
"A modern Greek tragedy about love foredoomed, family
life as battlefield, [and] the wisdom and wantonness
of the human heart."—*Kirkus*
288 pp • $14.95 • ISBN: 978-1-933372-10-5

Gene Kerrigan
The Midnight Choir
"The lethal precision of his closing punches leave
quite a lasting mark."—*Entertainment Weekly*
368 pp • $14.95 • ISBN: 978-1-933372-26-6

Little Criminals
"A great story...relentless and brilliant."—Roddy Doyle
352 pp • $16.95 • ISBN: 978-1-933372-43-3

Peter Kocan
Fresh Fields
"A stark, harrowing, yet deeply courageous work
of immense power and magnitude."—*Quadrant*
304 pp • $14.95 • ISBN: 978-1-933372-29-7

The Treatment and The Cure
"A little masterpiece, not only in the history of prison
literature, but in that of literature itself."—*The Bulletin*
256 pp • $15.95 • ISBN: 978-1-933372-45-7

Helmut Krausser
Eros
"Helmut Krausser has succeeded in writing a great
German epochal novel."—*Focus*
352 pp • $16.95 • ISBN: 978-1-933372-58-7

Carlo Lucarelli
Carte Blanche
"Lucarelli proves that the dark and sinister
are better evoked when one opts for unadulterated
grit and grime."—*The San Diego Union-Tribune*
128 pp • $14.95 • ISBN: 978-1-933372-15-0

The Damned Season
"One of the more interesting figures
in crime fiction."—*The Philadelphia Inquirer*
128 pp • $14.95 • ISBN: 978-1-933372-27-3

Via delle Oche
"Lucarelli never loses his perspective on human nature
and its frailties."—*The Guardian*
160 pp • $14.95 • ISBN: 978-1-933372-53-2

Edna Mazya
Love Burns
"Combines the suspense of a murder mystery with
the absurdity of a Woody Allen movie."—*Kirkus*
224 pp • $14.95 • ISBN: 978-1-933372-08-2

Sélim Nassib
I Loved You for Your Voice
"Nassib spins a rhapsodic narrative out of the indissoluble
connection between two creative souls inextricably
bound by their art."—*Kirkus*
272 pp • $14.95 • ISBN: 978-1-933372-07-5

The Palestinian Lover
"A delicate, passionate novel in which history and
life are inextricably entwined."—*RAI Books*
192 pp • $14.95 • ISBN: 978-1-933372-23-5

Alessandro Piperno
The Worst Intentions
"A coruscating mixture of satire, family epic, Proustian
meditation, and erotomaniacal farce."—*The New Yorker*
320 pp • $14.95 • ISBN: 978-1-933372-33-4

Benjamin Tammuz
Minotaur
"A novel about the expectations and compromises that humans create for
themselves...Very much in the manner of William Faulkner and Lawrence
Durrell."—*The New York Times*
192 pp • $14.95 • ISBN: 978-1-933372-02-0

Chad Taylor
Departure Lounge
"There's so much pleasure and bafflement to be derived from
this thriller by novelist Chad Taylor."—*The Chicago Tribune*
176 pp • $14.95 • ISBN: 978-1-933372-09-9

Roma Tearne
Mosquito
"A lovely, vividly described novel."—*The Times* (London)
352 pp • $16.95 • ISBN: 978-1-933372-57-0

Christa Wolf
One Day a Year
"This remarkable book offers insight into the mind behind
the public figure."— *The New Yorker*
640 pp • $16.95 • ISBN: 978-1-933372-22-8

Edwin M. Yoder Jr.
Lions at Lamb House
"Yoder writes with such wonderful manners, learning,
and detachment."—William F. Buckley Jr.
256 pp • $14.95 • ISBN: 978-1-933372-34-1

www.europaeditions.com

Michele Zackheim
Broken Colors
"A profoundly original, beautifully written work, so emotionally accurate
that it tears at the heart. I read it without stopping."
—Gerald Stern
320 pp • $14.95 • ISBN: 978-1-933372-37-2

Children's Illustrated Fiction

Altan
Here Comes Timpa
48 pp • $14.95 • ISBN: 978-1-933372-28-0

Timpa Goes to the Sea
48 pp • $14.95 • ISBN: 978-1-933372-32-7

Fairy Tale Timpa
48 pp • $14.95 • ISBN: 978-1-933372-38-9

Wolf Erlbruch
The Big Question
52 pp • $14.95 • ISBN: 978-1-933372-03-7

The Miracle of the Bears
32 pp • $14.95 • ISBN: 978-1-933372-21-1

(with **Gioconda Belli**)
The Butterfly Workshop
40 pp • $14.95 • ISBN: 978-1-933372-12-9